# THE FIESTA BURGER MURDER

## MURDER

*A Burger Bar Mystery Book* 1

## ROSIE A. POINT

**Join my no-spam newsletter and receive an exclusive offer. Details can be found at the back of this book.**

**Cover by DLR Cover Designs**
**www.dlrcoverdesigns.com**

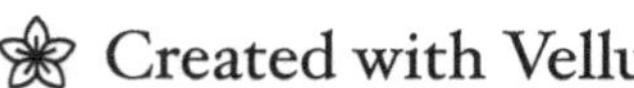 Created with Vellum

# YOU'RE INVITED!

Hi there, reader!

I'd like to formally invite you to join my awesome community of readers. We love to chat about cozy mysteries, cooking, and pets.

It's super fun because I get to share chapters from yet-to-be-released books, fun recipes, pictures, and do giveaways with the people who enjoy my stories the most.

So whether you're a new reader or you've been

enjoying my stories for a while, you can catch up with other like-minded readers, and get lots of cool content by visiting my website at *www.rosiepointbooks.com* and signing up for my mailing list.

Or simply search for me on *www.bookbub.com* and follow me there.

I look forward to getting to know you better.

Let's get into the story!

Yours,
Rosie

❈   I   ❈

leepy Creek had a million secrets.

Some secrets drifted below the surface like crispy French fries trapped in a well of oil, others were as juicy as a sumptuous beefy burger. Those were the secrets that intrigued me the most.

Maybe that was the hunger talking.

I hadn't eaten since I'd gotten on the bus, hours ago.

This place was simultaneously snooze-ville and the friendliest town in the Midwest. With gossip and lies for seasoning.

I adjusted the straps of my backpack and strode away from the bus. "Here we go again."

I hadn't planned on coming back to my hometown when I'd left years ago—which sane woman would come back after what this place had put me through? Being back here brought back way too many memories.

*Don't go there.*

But now, I didn't have much of a choice. I *had* to be here.

"Guess it's time eat my weight in burgers and fries," I muttered. Emotional eating for the win, right?

"Talking to yourself, dear?" An old lady hopped off the grated steps of the bus and came over. "You know what they say about that, don't you?"

"It's the first sign of insanity?"

"No, no. It's a sign of clinical loneliness," she said.

I blinked and shook my head. Typical Sleepy Creek.

"You should get a cat," the woman continued. "Did you know they're capable of eating an entire human being? A dead one, of course."

"Uh, what?"

"It's true. I saw it on that Discovery Channel."

"Who are you?" I scanned her lined cheeks. She had a speck of chocolate on her bottom lip.

"I'm Missi, dear, short for Mississippi," she replied. "Cats are good housekeepers. If you die while you're here you won't have to worry about the clean-up."

"I'm thirty," I said, because how on earth was I supposed to respond to that?

"Accidents happen." Missi winked then shuffled off, her silver curls bobbling atop her head.

Yeah, I definitely didn't like being back here. Any other town in Ohio would've been fine, but here—

"Christie?"

I spotted my friend outside the windows

of an old-timey lookin' barber shop, complete with a striped barber's pole.

Her blonde hair was tied back, and an escaped strand hung loose next to her ear. That hair had a kink in it, but not from a hair tie. It was from a pillow.

She'd overslept.

My gaze flicked over the lipstick smudged in the right corner of her mouth, then to the clump of mascara on her left eyelid.

"I did call ahead to give you enough time," I said.

"I—uh?" My blast from the past high school best friend, Grizzy, frowned. "Huh?"

"You overslept."

"How did you know? Wait, you're doing that thing again, aren't you? That Sherlock Holmes thing."

Ugh, Grizzy knew I hated that reference. I'd read a lot of crime novels growing up because of my mother's obsession with them. It was the reason she'd named me Christie. After Agatha Christie, of course.

"Attention to detail." I shrugged off my backpack. "How are you?" She was tired, obviously. It'd be rude to point that out, though.

"I'm good. But what does that matter?" Grizzy grasped my forearm and half-walked, half-dragged me down the sidewalk, past groups of elderly citizens and young mothers out bright and early.

The old folks because sleep had eluded them, and the mother's for the same reason but a different cause: the screaming babies. Poor souls.

"Where are we going?" I asked.

"To talk. We haven't talked in what, like, ten years? I need to get a good look at you."

I wrinkled my nose. "It's been two days since we last Skyped, Griz."

"That's not the same thing and you know it." She stopped in front of her restaurant and relinquished her grip on me. She rammed her fists onto her hips. "What happened?"

"You mean, apart from my unending

hunger for one of your burgers? Nothing." I didn't want to tell her what'd happened.

"Liar."

"I'm serious."

"Why did you take a break from work? You love Boston. You love your job."

"Loved," I said. "Loved it. Past tense."

Understanding flashed across her face. "Oh. Oh, no. I'm sorry, Chris. I'm real sorry about that."

"It's not your fault." It was mine.

I had overstepped the line when I'd questioned a witness. The only witness in a murder trial who happened to be a senator's daughter. After ten years as a homicide detective with the department I hadn't been offered a promotion. I hadn't led an investigation, though I'd solved countless cases.

I was my own worst enemy. Too impulsive. That was the phrase the Captain had used.

Well, boo hockey to that. I wouldn't let a hiccup like this slow me down.

"Chris?"

"Yeah," I said. "I zoned out for a second there, didn't I?"

The pity on my best friend's face made my cheeks hot.

"You want a burger? On the house." Grizzy gestured to the restaurant. Its sign glimmered against the bricks overhead.

"Grizzy's Burger Bar—Guaranteed Best Grilled Burgers in Sleepy Creek," I said.

"And don't you forget it." She grinned. "Come on. I've got the Mexican Fiesta special going at the moment. You'll love it." Grizzy pushed into the interior of her restaurant, and I followed her, ignoring the curiosity of the diners and the information assaulting my senses.

I was back. And my conscience prodded me—the niggling voice in the back of my mind I despised. It wanted me to investigate the one case I'd sworn I'd never touch.

My mother's murder.

✣    2    ✣

"**P**ull up a chair, gorgeous," Grizzy said, and patted a stool in front of the long counter at the back of the diner.

I slid onto it and caught a glimpse of my reflection in the mirror that spanned the wall opposite. Oh heavens, I had to get a haircut. Those loose tendrils of dark brown hair had too many split ends to count. Back in Boston, I'd lost my girly habits.

I'd conditioned but never styled. And nail polish? Forgettaboutit. The only thing I'd refreshed regularly was my trusty tube of mascara. My mother had maintained that a flick of mascara on the lashes was a woman's best weapon.

The habit had stuck, though I didn't agree with the sentiment.

Grizzy whipped out a soda glass and prepared my favorite drink. A root beer float. "So?"

"So." I shrugged off my bag. I dropped it to the tiles.

The store's warm atmosphere curled around my shoulders and eased the tension from the long bus ride. Chatter, along with the clinking of glasses and plates, punctuated the hum from the coffee machine.

"Come on, give me the scoop." Grizzy tinged a bell on the counter in the window to the right of the counter.

A man with a shining face appeared and scrutinized her. He shoved his chef's hat to one side. "What's happenin?" He had a thick Jamaican accent.

"I need a Mexican Fiesta, Jarvis," Grizzy said.

The man lifted a maraca, rattled it, then grinned. "Comin' right up, mon."

"I—uh—what did you ask me again, Griz?"

"The scoop, Chris, the scoop. I know you're on the outs with your job now, but what's the deal?"

"I pushed a little too hard, a little too fast," I said. "And yeah, they suspended me."

"Oh, thank heavens." Grizzy slid the root beer float onto the polished countertop. "I thought it was over for good."

"If it was over for good I wouldn't have come back here."

"Why *did* you come back?"

"I had free time," I replied, and focused on the blob of vanilla ice cream floating in a sea of fizz. "It was about time I paid you a visit, know what I mean?"

"Uh huh, uh huh. I'm not buying it," she said. Out of the two of us, Griselda was the less perceptive one, and that meant I wasn't being discreet.

"C'mon, Griz."

"Don't you, 'c'mon, Griz,' me, Christie Lilith Watson," she said. "I know why you're back, and it's got nothing to do with me. It's the case, isn't it?"

The case was the invisible presence chasing me around and forcing me onward and upward. It had driven me to take my detective's test. To graduate at the top of my class from police academy before that.

"We shouldn't talk about it here," I said.

"Ha, I knew it. You're going to investigate it, aren't you?" Grizzy whispered. "That's the real reason you drove out here."

"I didn't drive," I said, and poked the ice cream with my straw. "I bussed."

"Now you're avoiding the question."

I was torn about investigating what had happened to my mom. I'd carried it around with me for twelve years. I didn't want to deal with that on my break, but I craved answers. They had never solved my mom's case.

Grizzy pursed her lips at me, but I didn't give her a response. "Suit yourself, then. But this isn't the end of it, woman. If you're going to live under my roof, it's going to be by my rules. And that means no secrets."

I snorted.

"I'm serious. And you're going to earn your keep. You're going to be a server in the Burger Bar."

"Is that how you plan on keeping me out of trouble?" I asked. "You know that will only cause more drama." I'd never been a 'people person' and she knew it.

"You said you're suspended," Grizzy replied. "And that means you've got to behave yourself."

She was right. I'd had my hearing and they'd determined I needed a three-month sabbatical with pay. They'd review my psychological health after that period. Captain Wilkes had practically shoved me out of the door, but not before he'd warned me that I was to stay out of trouble and out of investigations or, "You're toast, Watson."

"Griz, I—"

The bell tinged, and Jarvis reappeared. He placed a red basket, complete with a checked napkin, on the counter top. "Mexican Fiesta Burger, mon." He rattled the colorful maracas again.

"Thank you," I called out.

Grizzy swept the basket over and placed it in front of me. "After you're done, we'll head back to my place and get you settled. Sound good?"

"I could go on my own."

Grizzy exhaled, reminding me of a horse flapping its lips. "Don't start with that. We've got a lot of catching up to do. Besides, Jarvis's cousin Martin is coming in for his shift in a half an hour. I'm free after that."

"If you're sure." I didn't want to be too much trouble. Just because I had a "vacation" didn't mean I could roll into Sleepy Creek and upset her schedule.

"Duh." Grizzy winked at me.

I turned my attention to the meal. The tower of meat, melted cheese and soft, sesame speckled buns induced a flood of drool. Gosh, I'd forgotten my hunger for a second there. "This smells amazing."

"Don't get your hopes up," a man spoke, behind me.

The man's viciously hooked nose suited the snarl in his tone. He was crane tall with terrible posture—hunching over so that his neck scooped forward. His left eyelid drooped. Medical disorder? Stroke?

He twitched into the chair next to mine. "That," he said, and pointed at the burger, "is a one way ticket to the bathroom. You mark my words. You'll regret it later."

"Good morning, Paul," Grizzy said, in a long-suffering tone. "What can I get you?"

"Who puts jalapeños on a burger, huh?

What kind of crazy lady thinks that's a good idea?"

I took off the burger's bun and studied the jalapeño relish on top. "Looks good to me."

"Stay out of trouble," Captain Wilkes had said. And that was exactly what I intended to do. But if he insulted Grizzy again I might forget about good behavior and decorate him with the relish instead of eating it.

"What do *you* know?" Paul sneered at me. "You're an out-of-towner, ain't ya? Never seen you around here before. Little Miss Nobody. Little Miss Jalapeño Lover."

"The manners in this town have taken a dive." I popped the top of my burger bun back into place.

"What you know about manners, out-of-towner?" Paul asked, smoothing tapered fingers over his bald crown. "You smell like bus and smog."

"Anything's better than," I paused, leaned in and sniffed, "cat urine. Is that cat urine?"

Paul scrambled off his seat, all arms and

legs like an overgrown spider. The chatter in the restaurant hushed as the customers turned to watch the show. "Little woman, you'd better take that back or I'll—"

"That's enough." Usually, the musical quality of Grizzy's voice would've fit into a choir, but now, she'd gone rough around the edges. "That's more than enough. Paul, I won't stand for you upsetting my customers and my guests. I'm going to have to ask you to leave."

"And what if I don't go?" Paul asked.

The silver kitchen door swung open, and Jarvis ambled up. "We gotta problem?" He folded his meaty arms across his chest, and his biceps strained against the short sleeves of his chef's shirt. The end of a spatula poked out of his massive fist.

Spider Paul's gaze swept over Jarvis. He paled and narrowed his eyes at Grizzy. "You'll regret this, missy. You hear me. You'll regret this." He gave Jarvis another once-over, then clattered out into the street.

Under different circumstances I would've

flashed him my badge and asked him if he deemed verbal threats appropriate. Shoot, I might've pulled him into the station for a chat about disturbing the peace.

Grizzy clapped her hands. "All right, show's over everybody. Get back to your Fiestas and Double Cheeses."

"Don't forget the Breakfast Burger," a man called out. A few customers chuckled, and the noise resumed, a slow swell of sound that rushed to fill the spaces Paul had created.

"Loopy Paul giving you trouble again, Griselda?" The woman I'd met at the bus sat on the stool Paul had vacated. She nodded but didn't recognize me. Her voice was deeper, and wait, hadn't that Missi woman's hair been silver not purple?

"Hey, Virginia," Griz said.

So she wasn't Missi. Had Sleepy Creek upgraded from secrets to cloning its inhabitants? I took a bite of my burger.

Grizzy offered the elderly woman a smile

and continued, "You know Paul. Always causing a fuss. What can I get for you?"

"I'll take a Mexican Fiesta, dear."

"Comin' right up."

"One second, one second." Jarvis shot back into the kitchen and grabbed his maraca.

I got the distinct impression that my vacation in Sleepy Creek would be anything but peaceful. But with a burger to eat and the warmth of the restaurant enveloping me, I wasn't too worried about it.

❧     3     ❧

"Are you sure about this?" I asked. "I could get a hotel room. It wouldn't be a problem."

"Whatever," Grizzy replied. "Like I'll let you camp out in Sleepy Creek Motel. I mean, we're on the map but it's all moth-eaten sheets and brown stains on the mattresses."

"Gross."

"Exactly. Besides, I haven't seen you in years. This will give us the perfect opportunity to catch up." Grizzy unlocked the front door of her house.

I stifled a yawn, the cool evening breeze grazing the back of my neck. We'd walked to Grizzy's place from the Burger Bar and caught sight of the town's highlights shrouded by the dark or highlighted by wrought iron streetlamps.

The Sleepy Creek Park, Public Library, and the old town hall that had been converted into a youth center, offset by the chirp of crickets. Then we'd entered suburbia and the landmarks had been replaced by lit windows and the scent of home cooking.

Grizzy led me into her two story—it had belonged to her grandmother—then double locked the front door behind us. "You can never be too careful."

"It's Sleepy Creek. What could possibly happen?" My mother's case was an exception that proved the rule in this town. It was quiet and friendly. Still full of gossips and secrets, and the occasional theft, but that was about it.

My friend shrugged. "Let's get you settled

in. I've got a guest room on the second floor with your name on it. Not literally, but it's outfitted in pink frills and flowers."

"You're kidding," I said.

"I know how much you love girly stuff." The sarcasm was strong with this one.

"Hey, I do my nails." I hid them in my pockets—between the bus ride and the dismissal, I hadn't had a chance to do anything but nibble on them.

"This way."

I hefted my bag and followed her up the stairs into the pinkest guest room on the planet. Fake roses in a pearlescent vase, a pine four poster bedecked in a flowery bedspread —oh heavens. "You weren't kidding." I dropped my bag next to the bed. "Grizzy, this is super kind of you."

"What are friends for? Besides, you'll be paying me back by working in the Burger Bar."

I laughed. "You realize I might end up chasing customers off."

"You give yourself too little credit," she said. "What, with a cute butt and a sweet smile like yours?"

I kept a straight face to make a point.

"I'm only kidding." Grizzy sat down on the edge of the bed, the mattress squeaking, and slotted her fist under her chin.

"Uh oh. What's this about?" I gestured to her.

"It's my 'worry' pose," she said. "Are you sure you're OK?"

Ever since I'd been suspended for my behavior I'd been on edge. Being a detective was my life, but this was a sabbatical. That was all.

"I'm fine," I said. "I can't throw a pity party when I'm the one to blame for my problems."

"You're allowed to be upset, though. You're not a bionic woman, although sometimes I wonder."

I walked to the bedroom window, and then leaned against the lurid wallpaper, scanning Grizzy's dark back yard. Back in Boston, this view would've given me the creeps—anyone could be watching—but this was Sleepy Creek. I'd bank on stray cats and nothing else.

I caught my best friend's worried reflection in the window. "What about you?" I asked. "Seriously, enough about me. You're a huge success. That burger nearly killed me it was so good."

"Oh, that's all Jarvis. He's a genius in the kitchen. The bar was doing fine before he came on board but we took off after he started. I don't know what I'd do without him."

"Are you two—uh, you know?"

"Dating?" Grizzy burst out laughing. "No way. He's happily married, he's as cuddly as a teddy bear and like a brother to me."

He hadn't seemed cuddly in the restaurant after Loopy Paul had caused trouble.

"What about—?" A *crash* outside cut me off. My muscles went taut as line on the end of a fishing pole.

"What was that?" Grizzy whispered.

I held up a palm. A low moan drifted up from the darkened garden. Another crash and then a thump.

"Turn off the light," I said.

Grizzy clicked it off.

Two shapes took form at the end of the garden, next to Grizzy's slatted wood fence. One was low, unmoving, and the other crouched over it. Was it a man and a dog? No, Grizzy hadn't mentioned a dog. And a dog would've barked at an intruder.

"What is it?" Grizzy squeaked off the bed.

I didn't answer. I opened the sash window and slid it into place as quietly as possible.

The second shape quit moving. They were ... listening?

I braced my palms on the sill and leaned out, listening right back.

The figure leaped up and grabbed the fence—the boards rattled and shoes bonked against wood. They were making a run for it!

"Hey!" I yelled. "Stop right there."

The shadow slipped over the top of the fence and out of sight.

"What was that?" Grizzy asked.

"I don't know," I replied. "Does Sleepy Creek have a resident ghost?" It wasn't a serious question, of course.

"No. Unless you're talking about Old Timer Earl. But no one's seen his ghost since Milly passed," she replied.

That was too much to process. "You need to call the cops. Now."

"But—why?"

"I'd bet my badge that's a dead body."

"Please tell me you're joking."

I drew myself back into the room and cracked the top of my head on the window's edge. "Ouch."

"A dead body?" Grizzy fanned her face, wafting the icy air over to me. "A dead body? No, no. That's not—it can't be. Why?"

"Stop panicking. I'm going downstairs to see for myself. You call 911. OK?" I took her by the shoulders and jiggled her. "OK?"

"No, it's not OK. I'm scared. I'm on the verge of expelling everything from both ends."

"That's—uh, that's something, Grizzy."

"I'm serious."

"Relax, Griz. It's all under control. But we're not going to find out what's going on by staying up here. Trust me. I've done this before, remember?" I patted her shoulder. "Call 911." I had to get down there. If there was a dead body in my friend's yard I was obligated to work this out. It sounded like an excuse. I wasn't supposed to get involved—my badge was at stake—but the itch to find out what had happened was back.

I jogged down the stairs and into the kitchen, found the light switches and flicked them up.

Light flared, and I squinted, making for the back door. Grizzy had triple locked this one. Her footsteps creaked overhead, and muffled chatter, panicked, of course, drifted through the ceiling. She'd called 911, at last.

I finally got the back door open. Light

from the porch's single bulb danced across the grass and illuminated the body, face down, in a washed-out haze. It took me a minute to cross the yard. The shape grew clearer—spindly arms and legs, and a trench coat.

"Loopy Paul." So much for my excitement-free sabbatical.

❧ 4 ❧

The lanky jalapeño hater was dead.

I'd checked his vitals, scanned for signs of a head injury, and attempted CPR by the time the ambulance and the cops had arrived. But Loopy Paul was gone. He'd lost too much blood from the stab wound beneath his sternum.

Paramedics flooded the scene, and I backed off to let them do their job. It wasn't my place to get involved. This wasn't Boston, and I wasn't an official even if that desire to find justice had already kicked me in the pants.

"Omigosh." Grizzy hovered on the porch, digging her manicured nails into her cheeks. "Christie, is that—?"

"It's him," I said. "It's Loopy Paul."

"Paul Whitmore," a man spoke nearby. "That's his full name."

The voice reminded me of an Old Spice advert, and the face matched it. A handsome —I had never used that term lightly—detective waited at the base of the stairs.

Wrinkles around the eyes, a little older than I was, no gray in the hair, and a jaw that could chop down trees. All right, so I'd exaggerated that last part, but he *did* have a chin dimple.

"You need to ask us questions," I said. "Take our statements?"

"That's correct," he said. "I'm Detective Balle. I don't recognize you. You new to town?"

"You could say that." I folded my arms.

"She's visiting from Boston."

I stopped myself from poking Grizzy in the ribs. I didn't want handsome guy detective scrounging around in my recent past.

"Boston, eh?" Detective Balle raised an eyebrow. "You don't sound like you're from there."

I shrugged.

"What's your name?"

"Christie," I said.

He brought out a pen and a notepad. "Last name?"

"Watson."

"Elementary, my dear Watson." Another detective appeared. Mussed hair, six-foot-two, little extra around the middle, but no slouch. Remains of dinner on his collar. Was that a smear of ketchup?

He'd eaten in a rush. Ugh, Grizzy was right. I had to stop with the Sherlock Holmes stuff.

"Hi Arthur." Griselda was out of breath. I'd never seen my best friend go doe-eyed over a guy before, but she did a great impression of a smitten high-schooler, apparently.

"Griselda," the second detective said, and went pink. "I liked the special today. Those jalapeños had a real kick."

"It's all Jarvis. He's the genius behind the flavors," she said.

Detective Balle coughed and both of them blushed.

"Sorry, Liam," the second detective said.

"Miss Watson, this is Detective Cotton. He'll take Miss Lewis's statement while—"

"You're kidding, right?" I bit my bottom lip.

"I don't kid often," Liam Balle replied. "What are you talking about?"

"He's Detective Cotton. You're Detective Balle. Cotton. Balle?" It was the funniest combination of partner names I'd heard in a while and working up in Boston I'd heard a couple doozeys. Literally. The Doozey brothers had worked homicide for ages—they'd created a legacy.

The detectives exchanged a quizzical glance—they didn't get the joke.

"Oh, come on." I flopped my hands. "Cotton. Ball. Cotton ball?" They didn't crack a smile. "Never mind."

"Miss Watson, if you'll come with me, we can talk about what you witnessed this evening," Detective Balle said.

His partner led Grizzy inside the house and out of earshot.

I sat down on the porch swing and Detective Balle lowered himself into the spot next to me. The seat was cramped, and our thighs touched. I shifted to give him more space. He did the same for me.

"Miss Watson."

"Please, call me Christie," I said. "Miss Watson is too formal." And it reminded me of my mother.

"Christie, I'm going to ask you questions about what happened this evening and then I'm going to take your statement," Balle said. "Are you onboard with that?"

"Of course." I'd never stand in the path of justice.

"Let's start from the beginning. When did you become aware that Mr. Whitmore was in the backyard?"

"Not until I ran down," I replied. "But I was aware there was someone here before that. Two people."

"Two people." He kept his face impassive, but those broad shoulders tensed underneath his buttoned shirt. "Two intruders?"

"Yeah. Grizzy and I were upstairs in the guest bedroom when we heard a noise. A sharp crash. There were other noises too. Thumps," I said. "I proceeded to the window to assess the situation and discovered two shadowy figures at the back fence."

"You proceeded. You assessed the situation," the detective said. "Miss—Christie are you in law enforcement?"

Great. My professional lingo and stiff attitude had let the monkey out of the bag. "Boston P.D. Homicide."

"Oh," he said, and deflated a little.

Boston was big city. Sleepy Creek was small town. A lot of times, the guys from the big city made the small-towners feel, well, small.

"Yeah, I'm on sabbatical," I said, and offered him a winning smile—so he'd know I wasn't like the other arrogant detectives. "No police work for me." Still, the case of the dead jalapeño hater intrigued me.

Detective Balle wrote a note on his pad. "What happened after you discovered the two shadowy figures by the back fence?"

"I told Grizzy to switch off the light so we could see them better." I tried to relax my professional lingo. "Then the first figure jumped over the fence and ran for it. After that I came down and Grizzy called 911. I tried to revive Paul, but it didn't work." I nodded to the covered stretcher wheeling past the side of the house, two paramedics on either side of it. "Unfortunately."

"Did you get a good look at the individual who jumped the fence?"

"No. And even if I had I wouldn't have recognized them," I said. "It's been a while since I last visited the Creek. Everyone's a new face." *His face is handsome.* Gosh, what a ridiculous thought. We were ten feet from a crime scene for heaven's sake.

"Did Miss Lewis ever mention Paul? Any arguments they might've had?" Balle asked.

I tensed up. "What? Why are you asking?" Of course, I knew why he'd asked. Paul's body had been found on Grizzy's property. It was natural that the detective would investigate that avenue. It made the hairs on the back of my neck stand up, though. Griselda wouldn't hurt a fly.

"I'm following leads, Miss—Christie."

"Grizzy has an alibi. She was upstairs with me." But my word didn't count for much.

"Please answer the question."

I sucked up my anger and told him about the run-in I had witnessed today, and that

Paul and Jarvis had also had a minor disagreement. He wrote it down, his expression blank.

"That's all the questions I have for now."

I grabbed Balle's arm. "Wait a second," I said. "Level with me here, detective. Are you going to investigate my friend? Me?"

Balle gave me icy professionalism in return, glancing down at my hand on his forearm. "Ma'am, I'm not at liberty to discuss an ongoing case."

Good cop. Pity. It would've been much easier to operate with a bad one in charge of the investigation.

And operate I would. If Grizzy was in danger of taking the fall for a murder she hadn't committed, I'd go to the ends of the Earth to prove her innocence.

Griselda Lewis was the only person who'd been there for me after Mom had died. It was time to return the favor.

## 5

Perhaps, I had overreacted about Detective Balle's investigation. Things were clearer in the light of day, especially from the inside of Grizzy's Burger Bar where the smells, and Jarvis's low humming from the kitchen, drove off negativity.

The combination of exhaustion, a long, sweaty bus drive, and my frustration at the sabbatical had added up. Just because a corpse had been found in my best friend's back yard didn't mean she would take the fall for the murder.

"Do you hear yourself, right now?" I muttered.

"Do you?"

I spun around, holding my empty delivery tray, and came face-to-face with none other than the cat lady. Or was it the woman Grizzy had called Virginia yesterday afternoon?

"Talking to yourself again, dear?" she asked, and patted her silver curls. "There's an animal shelter down the road."

"Missi," I said. "That's your name, correct?"

"Mississippi. Our mother's choose our names. It's a pity we can't choose our mothers, isn't it? How about you fetch me a Double Thick Chocolate Malt Shake? Oh, and tell that strapping chef I say hello, will you?"

"I—uh, OK?"

"Are you asking me or agreeing with me?"

"I'm agreeing with you?"

"You're doing it again," Missi said, and

clipped open her purse. She brought out a lipstick tube, then rolled out the plum colored wedge and gestured with it. "Chocolate Malt. Double Thick. Don't get it wrong, new girl." She sauntered off and took a seat in the corner booth.

Jarvis tinged the bell in the kitchen window. "Order up, mon."

"Coming." I rushed to the delivery section.

Though she was shaken over finding a dead customer in her yard, Grizzy had come into work with me this morning. She'd decided to hang back and work the milkshake and soda bar instead of dealing with the people. As if my dealing with them was an improvement.

"Are you ready?" Griselda brushed back her messy blonde hair. "The lunch hour rush is called a rush for a reason."

"I'm as ready as I can be, given the circumstances," I said. "Say, who's that Missi lady over in the corner? She wants a Double—"

"Thick Chocolate Malt Shake? Yeah, that's her regular drink order," Grizzy said. "I'll whip one up. She's one of the twins. Sleepy Creek's terrible twins."

"That's catchy." A lot had changed in the twelve years I'd been gone. When I'd lived here there had been a few terrible things— soggy bagels from the local bakery, gossip around every corner, and a statue of a pigeon covered in pigeon poop to name a few—but none of them had been twins.

"You get the idea," Grizzy replied. "Her sister was in here yesterday. Virginia? They were both named after the states their mother and father were born in. Virginia's the soft-spoken one and Missi—"

"Still has good hearing in a half-empty restaurant," the elderly woman called from the corner. "Are you going to milk the cow too?"

"Coming, coming." Grizzy grabbed ice cream from the silver freezer below the counter. "It's good to have you back, Missi."

"Is it? Sorry, dear, I'm a bit grumpy from

the trip." Missi folded her arms. "All that way for nothing."

"This milkshake will cheer you up."

I zoomed over to the kitchen and picked up the burger order—if I left it any longer, the hungry customer, skinny guy with a hand tattoo, would complain. I couldn't stand whining, and I hated bringing down the group average.

"Thanks Jarvis. Oh by the way, the lady over there says hello. Missi."

Jarvis winced. "Thanks."

"You want me to say hello back?"

He shook his head. "You say hello to that one and she gon' come over here. No mon, no way. You tell her I'm busy with the burgers."

"Got it." Did Missi have a crush on the strapping and very married chef? None of my business.

I whisked the burger over to tattoo-hand and delivered it without a smile. Not because I was crabby. I was more interested in Missi.

The regulars would have their ear to the ground. Their fingers on the languid pulse of the Creek. If anyone knew who'd killed Loopy Paul it'd be them. Truth be told, I couldn't shake the itch to investigate.

Shoot, it wasn't as if I'd go ahead and follow the leads. So what if I asked a few questions? This was for Grizzy.

"Lies, all lies," I muttered.

"What's that?" Tattoo Hand asked. The picture etched onto his skin drew my attention—a bug, spiked and swirled. He covered it and frowned at me.

"Sorry. Nothing. Enjoy your burger, sir." I left him to his meat and jalapeño tower and fetched Mississippi's shake from the counter. Jarvis had quit humming. The only sounds were the sizzle of meat and the occasional *flick-thwack* of the spatula.

I delivered the shake with my best attempt at a customer-friendly smile.

Missi ignored me and grabbed a straw from the dispenser at the end of the booth. She stripped back the paper, plopped the tube into the milky deliciousness, then gulped down half of it. "Ah, that's better," she said. "All right, now I'm in a better mood. Take a seat, dear."

"I can't," I said. "I've got to deliver the burgers."

"You've got time," Missi replied. "George over there won't be done with those jalapeños for another half hour."

It couldn't hurt to mingle with the locals. It would smooth my transition from stranger to mere out-of-towner. I plonked down opposite Missi and folded my hands on top of the table.

The elderly woman took a break from her milkshake and fixed me with a crystal blue stare. "You saw the body, yes?"

"What?"

"Loopy Paul," Mississippi hissed. "Rumor has it he was found dead in Griselda's back yard last night, and you were the one who found him." She ensured George wasn't eavesdropping with a glance.

"News travels fast."

"Gossip is Sleepy Creek's incarnation of the common cold, dear," Missi replied. "So? Is it true?"

"Yeah, it's true. He was stabbed."

"Stabbed. And in Grizzy's back yard." Missi looked ready to burst from frustration. "Why *her* yard? Everyone loves Grizzy. It doesn't make any sense."

"Maybe it was a fluke." But I didn't believe that.

"You're supposed to be a detective. It's your job to figure this out, you know. Grizzy's been good to this town. Before she took over the Burger Bar there was nowhere good to eat and we didn't have any tourism to speak of. Now, we're booming and the food here has never been better. Oh, no, we can't let this slide. We can't let this slide."

Who was 'we?' "It's not my job to investigate anything. I'm on sabbatical. My only job is to bus tables and deliver food and drinks."

"Scintillating." She sighed, and we fell into an uneasy silence. "Paul Whitmore had enemies." Missi spoke out of the corner of her mouth. "He had so many of them that the cops will have their hands full tracking them down, mark my words."

"Enemies? Like who?"

"Enemies like his popular sister. Frances Sarah Dawkins. You remember that name. You remember it and you keep an eye out for her and her husband."

"I—"

"They fought with Paul a lot."

"Why?" I couldn't help myself.

"Rumor has it Paul had a lot of money and Frances Sarah and her husband, Pete, wanted it. Weird thing is, both her and her husband are rich. They're hosting the Spring Charity Ball tomorrow evening to raise money for their sleep apnea charity. Bleh. Sleep apnea, please."

"That's nice of them."

"Is it?" Missi asked. "*Is it?* I don't think they're as innocent as they seem. I'd bet my last mint they have a hidden agenda."

The glass front door—the smiling burger logo splashed across its front—opened and the purple-haired version of Missi entered. She spotted us and came over, swinging a tote bag large enough to hide several animals and, possibly, a murder weapon. "Is my sister giving you trouble, dear?"

"No. But I do have to get back to work." I slipped out of the booth and made way for Virginia.

"Remember what I told you, new girl," Missi said. "The Dawkins Charity Ball."

"Do I want to know what this is about?" Virginia arranged herself in the booth and placed her bag on the tabletop. "More conspiracies?"

"It's not a conspiracy. It's the search for the truth."

Virginia huffed. "You shush and drink your milkshake." She turned to me and smiled. "I'll have what she's having, dear. If you'd be so kind? But the vanilla version."

If that wasn't a metaphor then I didn't know what was. "Coming right up."

I collected George's empty basket then headed to the counter to give Grizzy the shake order. We made small talk, and I laughed through it all, but I couldn't rid myself of the buzzing questions.

Who had killed Loopy Paul? And why had they done it in my best friend's back yard?

## 6

The rest of the afternoon passed without incident—apart from when a customer who to be rushed a glass of milk after biting into a particularly spicy jalapeño.

Grizzy and I walked home together, the purple hour settling on our shoulders, and a cold wind urging us onward.

I'd spent the choking-customer free portion of the day mulling over options. The name Frances Sarah Dawkins had circled my mind, thought fin poking above the waters with the *Jaws* soundtrack playing on repeat in the background.

What if she was the murderer? Money was a common motivation. Apart from passion or rage or—all the other motivations I'd encountered in my tenure as a failing homicide detective.

The charity ball interested me, but I couldn't bring it up without rousing Grizzy's suspicion. *Eh, I should let the whole thing go, anyway.* Keep my head down and focus on serving burgers while Jarvis rattled his maracas and unsuspecting Ohioans choked on relish.

I raked my fingers through my hair, snagging them on a few knots. I hadn't heard from any of the detectives back home. None of them cared enough to call me, not Watkins or Jones. Not even the Doozey brothers.

"I need to get cat food," Grizzy said, and halted a couple houses down from her place. "Shoot, I totally forgot."

"Cat food? For what?"

"For Curly." Griselda wrinkled her nose. "She didn't come in last night. It was probably because of the commotion outside."

"That's one way of putting it. Wait, you have a cat? When did you get a cat?" I asked.

"Are you kidding me?" Grizzy gaped at me. "I talk about her all the time. Every time we Skype I tell you about her."

I clicked my fingers. "Curly, Curly. Wait, do you mean Carly?"

"No. Curly." Grizzy's shoulders shook as she held back a laugh.

"Oh, it's not Carly? I assumed you were talking about one of your customers or a really annoying neighbor."

"An annoying neighbor who steals kibble?" Grizzy asked.

"It's Sleepy Creek." I shrugged. "I'll believe anything you say when it comes to this place." We *had* discovered a dead body in her back yard last night. "Grizzy, I—"

"Oh. It's Detective Balle," my friend said.

The man himself strolled toward us, the

picture of calm control. "Good evening, Miss Lewis, Miss—Christie."

"I feel like Scarlett O'Hara when you do that," I said.

"How are you ladies this evening?" Balle blew past my comment.

"Tired," Grizzy said. "It's been a rough day and neither of us got much sleep. What can we help you with, detective?"

"Nothing in particular." Liam Balle had a heart-melting smile. I refused to be touched by it. Why would the homicide detective have returned if not to assess the scene of the crime?

They'd already cordoned off Grizzy's back yard, and we weren't allowed to go out there or break the seal they'd placed over the back door. It was only through the grace of detectives Cotton and Balle that we'd been permitted to remain in the house in the first place.

"You need to talk to us again?" I asked.

"No."

I scanned the street and the houses with lights on in their windows. "You were interviewing potential witnesses," I said.

"Ma'am, I'm not—"

"Yeah, yeah. I know." I waved a hand. "My guess is you were interviewing Griselda's neighbors. They would have had the best chance of witnessing the crime last night." Strings connected, but there were plenty of loose ends wriggling around. I grasped at them but they slipped from my fingers. I didn't have enough information. I shouldn't have *any* information.

"Miss Lewis," Liam said.

I switched back to him.

"I'm going to need to talk to you in the morning. Alone," he continued. "Detective Cotton will swing by to pick you up."

"This is highly unorthodox," I said. "Why not talk to her now?"

"I want Miss Lewis to have forewarning. I understand she has a business to run and I don't want to disturb her daily routine." Nice guy Balle. Huh, I wouldn't have pegged him as a man who cared about inconveniencing others on the course to justice.

We were polar opposites in that regard. Balle gave my friend forewarning about an interview. I crashed into witnesses' homes to interview them unannounced. That was the reason Balle had a job, and I didn't.

"Thank you," Grizzy said. "Thank you for the forewarning. I appreciate that. I'll call Martin and ask him to take the shift tomorrow morning. How long will the interview take?"

"I can't say, ma'am," Liam replied, formally.

I held back on rolling my eyes. *Why does he bother me so much? Gosh.*

"Thanks, Detective Balle." Grizzy started toward her house.

"Have a good evening," Liam said, and winked at me as I passed by.

What was that about? One second he was

the picture of cop goodness and the next he was—

"Chris?" Griselda was five steps ahead of me. "I'd like to get home and grab a bite to eat."

"Coming!" I glanced over my shoulder at the cop—his broad shoulders fading out of sight in the dusk—then hurried after my friend. I couldn't help considering each house we passed, peering through their front windows wherever curtains had been left open.

Someone must've seen something—why else would Balle have been in the area? He would have been honest if he'd been on Grizzy's property. And now he wanted to speak with her again?

Why hadn't I been called down to the station for another questioning about the night of the murder? Unless they had strong reason to suspect Grizzy had done it. Surely, a brief argument over jalapeños couldn't be considered motivation for murder.

"Curly," Grizzy said, and bent on the front path.

I'd been so caught up in my thoughts I hadn't realized we'd already arrived back home.

Griselda cradled a cat in her arms—a squat, black creature with a sharp face—and cooed. "Are you hungry Curly Fries? Are you hungry, gorgeous?"

"Curly Fries," I said.

"Of course. What else would I name her?"

"It's a girl?"

The cat *prrt-meowed* at me and flicked its tail. Ah, another enemy to add to the list. The ill intent shone in its yellow eyes. Curly Fries had already sized me up for future ingestion.

"Don't worry about her Curly. Come on, let's get you a bite to eat," Grizzy said, and smooshed her lips onto the creature's head. "I've got enough kibble for tonight, but we'll have to stop by the stove tomorrow."

"Don't forget me," I said, pointing at my stomach.

"I'll feed you once you've apologized to Curly. I want you two to make nice. If we have to live under the same roof we're going to do it peacefully."

I puffed out my cheeks and followed her up the front steps. "Sleepy Creek has a motel, right?"

$\mathscr{K}$  7  $\mathscr{K}$

Everywhere Grizzy went she carried that home style warmth. Her small kitchen embraced me. I loved that about my friend. The cat, however, was her polar opposite.

Curly Fries crunched kibble in the corner and spat moist chunks in every direction. She was the messiest eater I'd ever seen, and I'd witnessed one of the Doozey brothers destroy a bag of Reese's Pieces in under thirty seconds. The image had burned itself into my retinas.

"She's uh—cute." I took a seat at the hard-wood table.

"Be nice." Grizzy opened the fridge and brought out four eggs. "She's my only company, and I love her for it."

"Your only company? What about that strapping detective? The blonde one?"

Grizzy placed the eggs on the granite countertop and pretended she hadn't heard me. "How does an omelet sound? Grizzy's Go-To Omelet. It's my easy-peasy meal after a long day at work. Unless you want to order Chinese?"

"Don't avoid the question, Griselda," I said. "And yeah, an omelet sounds like heaven."

Grizzy busied herself in the cupboards. She hummed under her breath, and Curly Fries crunched away, cracking kibble between her vicious kitty teeth.

"Grizzy," I said.

"What?" She produced a glass bowl and whisk from the cupboard.

"You like him."

"Who?"

"Don't play dumb. You know who I'm talking about." I pierced her with my best investigative stare. "Arthur Cotton of Cotton and Balle. Those two should start a business together. That's a killer tagline."

"I—he's nice." Grizzy cracked two eggs into the bowl, one at a time, then whisked them. "He's a nice guy."

Griselda had been alone for a long time—her fiancé had left her and Sleepy Creek three years ago, and she'd never quite recovered. She didn't talk about emotional stuff, but she'd always been there for me, and darn it if I wouldn't return the favor.

"How nice of a guy is he?"

"Chris, it's not like that. I mean, it is, but it isn't. I'm not ready for anything serious. I'm still beat up over what happened with Bryan. How ridiculous is that?" she asked, and retrieved the ham, cheese, and mushrooms from the fridge.

"It's not ridiculous."

"It is," she said. "I've spent so much time recovering that I've forgotten how to live." She opened a drawer and brought out a cutting board and a knife. "I wake up in the morning, feed Curly Fries, go to the Burger Bar, work and socialize with the locals, go home, sleep. Repeat."

Griselda chopped up the ham, grated the cheese, then cut the mushrooms and placed them in a separate bowl. "And I know I shouldn't complain about my life. I have a better life than most people, and I appreciate that. I appreciate how far my restaurant has come and how great that part of my life is, but sometimes... I want more." She gestured with her knife and a bit of ham flicked off the end and plopped onto the tiles.

Curly Fries rushed forward and gobbled it up. Shockingly, she made the ham crunch too.

"I want to go out and meet new people. I want to be the person I used to be." She wiped the back of her hand over her forehead.

"Listen to me being selfish. A man was murdered in my back yard last night and all I can talk about is not having a social life."

"That's because it's been building up for a long time." Her mention of Loopy Paul gave me a brilliant idea. "I have a suggestion."

"Oh no." Grizzy adjusted the heat on the gas burner. "I don't want to get involved in anything to do with this murder. I've got enough to worry about already." Grizzy hadn't slept last night. Loopy Paul's death had freaked her out, and she had a mysterious meeting with the detectives to deal with in the morning.

"It's nothing like that," I said. "There's a charity ball tomorrow night. You must've heard about it from the customers at the Burger Bar."

"Yeah," Grizzy said. "I did, but I don't have anything to wear to a ball. And you're supposed to take a date."

"Tragedies abound," I replied. "Let's go together. I'll pick up a couple of dresses at one of the boutiques in town while you're having a chat with Arthur Cotton." I splashed his name in there as spice. "You know, he'll probably be there. Law enforcement officials are supposed to attend events like this. It makes the department appear caring—involved in the community."

"You're incorrigible." Grizzy didn't say no, though. She poured the eggs into the pan and they sizzled. She drew the mixture back, repeatedly.

"That smells great," I said. "But you didn't put milk in the mixture."

"Milk," she said. "Milk? Sacrilege. If you ever suggest that again I'll throw you out of my house. Do you hear me, Watson?"

"Loud and clear." Gosh, I was starved, and a day of serving burgers hadn't helped.

Grizzy finished my omelet, fed it onto a plate, then placed it on the table in front of me. "All right," she said. "We can do the charity ball thing. It might be fun."

"And it's for a good cause." I cut into my

omelet. The melted cheese oozed out of it, dotted with ham and mushrooms.

I speared a slice with my fork and ate it, savoring the heat, the flavors, everything. It was too good. "Divine." I ate another bite. "You're the best, Grizzy."

She set to work on her omelet. There were too many things bothering my friend. Tomorrow I'd get to the bottom of them, but for now I'd enjoy the omelet and ignore Curly Fries' hungry glare from the corner.

❧  8  ❧

The cat was a plague.

She'd jumped on my bed at 5:00 a.m. and kneaded the duvet, purring loud enough to rouse the dead. By the time I'd gotten down to the kitchen in full-on coffee zombie mode I'd progressed from grumpy to bad mood.

I whipped up a pot of coffee, poured myself a mug then headed out to Grizzy's front porch to enjoy the sunrise.

Morning coffee had to involve scenery, and the colder the temperature, the better—barring snow. The atmosphere helped awaken the senses.

Time ticked by and the sun rose, showing its orange face. The neighborhood woke up. Cars started, exhausts steamed, and children yelled or were commanded by their parents. Happy, suburban sounds that were foreign in comparison to the noises from my apartment back home.

I didn't miss the smog and horns and rush of cars. Or the arguments from my downstairs neighbors, the O'Malleys. Those two were worse than Grizzy's purring beast.

Speak of the devil, Curly Fries meandered out of the cat flap at around 6:30 a.m., after my second mug of the good stuff, and wound between my legs. She gave a terrific sneeze and splattered my bare feet with kitty spit.

"That's just lovely. Such a charmer." I waggled my foot.

"You know what they say about people who talk to themselves, right?" Grizzy had appeared in the doorway, wrapped in a fluffy white robe.

"Don't start."

"Still not a morning person, then? At least, that hasn't changed." She hid a yawn behind her mug. "How long have you been up?"

"You should ask Curly Fries that." I nudged the cat with my big toe. "She purred me awake. What about you, are you ready for the day? How are you feeling?"

Dark circles had appeared on the soft skin beneath my friend's eyes. "I'm as ready as I can be. I know the detectives need to get to the bottom of what happened but it makes me nervous. I already gave my statement, and they asked me questions when they were here the last time."

"What questions?" I kept my tone casual.

"No, you don't," Grizzy replied. "I'm not falling for that one, Christie Watson. You're not allowed to investigate anything or get involved in this kind of stuff."

"I wasn't—"

"Hush. I'm going upstairs to get dressed. Detective Cotton will be here soon."

"Don't forget to shave your legs," I replied.

"Cheap shot." Grizzy scooted off to get changed, and I studied the neighbor's houses instead, clasping the mug between my palms.

The houses on either side were similar to Grizzy's, though one had a wraparound porch and an annoying wind chime that *click-clocked* with every breath of air.

I'd have to do reconnaissance if I planned on figuring out who Detective Balle had talked to yesterday. And what they'd seen.

A police cruiser pulled up, and Detective Cotton got out. Clean shaven, a blob of what might've been shaving cream on his collar, and freshly ironed pants—someone wanted to impress Griselda.

Did these two realize that they both had crushes on each other?

"Morning," I said, and raised my mug. "Care for some coffee, detective?" *Care to give me some information?*

"Hi there, uh, Miss Watson."

"Good memory. Coffee?"

"No, thank you." Arthur brushed his palms down the front of his shirt. He chuckled. "I wish I could, but I've got to get Griselda down to the station for—"

The front door opened, and Grizzy clattered onto the porch, cheeks pink. She'd gussied up too—a pair of jeans and a smart, silk blouse. "Hello, Arthur."

"Griselda."

I hid the lower half of my face with my coffee cup. "I'll catch up with you later, Griz." After I'd done our dress shopping for the charity event.

"Yeah." Grizzy didn't make eye contact as she hurried down to meet Arthur.

The two lovebirds in denial drove off a minute later, car trailing exhaust fumes and the mix of Arthur's cologne and Grizzy's petalicious perfume—I'd bought that for her last birthday.

"Another day." My coffee had gone cold so

I placed the mug next to my foot and clasped my hands together instead.

Curly Fries tinkled out of the cat flap and down into the yard. She wormed between the bushes that hedged the fence, separating Grizzy's property from the neighbor's, and disappeared as only cats could.

I fixated on that spot. My vision had already hazed over, thoughts turning to Loopy Paul.

The man had obviously had enemies. But was his sister one of them? The charity ball tonight made me nervous. I didn't want to discover that Frances Sarah had been involved, because that would mean I'd want to investigate wholeheartedly.

But Grizzy, she was down at—

A *bang* brought me back to the present.

"You darn, cursed creature! Get out of here! Get out!"

I lurched out of my seat. The shouts had came from the house on the left. I craned my neck for a proper view of the man who had yelled.

He jogged down the front steps of his home, waving a broom—an old, witchy kind.

Bald spot on his crown, black, short hair around it. No shirt and a mess of chest hair above a distended belly. Holes in the knees of his pants. Messy dude. Might've been a recluse.

I tracked his path into the yard.

"Get out!" The neighbor brought down the straw broom and *whapped* the ground. "I'll—"

Curly Fries leaped over the fence, tail bottle-brush thick, and leaped into the bushes below.

"Hey!" I charged up to the border between the no-cat zone and home. "What the heck are you doing?"

Sweat streaked the neighbor dude's puffy face. "Who are you?"

"I'm one of Griselda's guests."

"*One* of them?"

"Her only guest," I corrected. "Why are you attacking her cat?"

"The darn thing is a nuisance. It jumped on my kitchen table and tried to eat the scrambled eggs off my plate." Neighbor guy wobbled the broom at Curly Fries, who'd settled on the porch behind us, licking her paws, unconcerned now that the excitement had passed.

Typical God-cat syndrome.

"Sorry," I said. "I didn't know she did stuff like that." Not that it was any excuse to swipe at her with a broom.

"Where's her mistress? She should be here to make sure that cat doesn't start terrorizing the neighborhood again."

Terrorizing was a strong word to use. So, Curly had a record in Sleepy Creek. "She's out."

"Out, huh? I saw that police car pass by. Did they arrest her for the murder of Loopy Paul? They're out of their minds if they think she did it," the guy said. "Hasn't got enough backbone."

"Griselda has plenty of backbone." This was the perfect segue. "But she's not a murderer. It's bad business though, that murder. I've only been in town a couple days, and I didn't expect to see that." I faked a shudder.

"Bad business," the neighbor agreed. He propped the broom against his hip and extended a hand. "Ray Tolentino."

I shook it. "Christie Watson." We parted, and I managed to wipe the sweat off my palm on my PJ pants, unseen. "Tell me something, Ray, did you see anything on the night it, uh, you know. The night Loopy Paul—"

"Got knifed," Ray replied. "Go ahead and say it. That was what happened."

"Did you see anything?"

"Why are you asking? You a cop?"

"No," I said. "I'm curious. I mean, it happened in my best friend's back yard. Obviously, I'm going to be alarmed. What if the killer comes back?" That same question rose

—*why* had it happened in Grizzy's back yard? Why there? The location couldn't be coincidental. It wasn't as if it was a back alley in a busy city.

Her place was flanked by two others and a row of houses at the back.

Ray leaned his chin on the top point of the broom's shaft. "I might've seen something," he said. "But I'm not the kind who gossips."

"Oh my gosh," I said, and pressed my palm to my chest—my feigned damsel in distress reaction. "Did you tell the police? What did you see?"

"I discussed it with them, yeah." Ray glanced over his left shoulder, his right, then leaned in. "It was a man."

"What?" I whispered. "How do you know?"

"Saw it with my own two peepers. See, I was up late watching TV, and I figured, why not make it a party? I have a stash of Mars Bars in my bedside table, so I went upstairs, and I heard this really weird noise."

"A crash?"

Ray clicked his fingers. "Exactly, yeah. So I took a gander outside, and a guy ran past my back fence."

"How do you know it was a guy?"

"Because he was taller than my fence. And it's six feet. Don't bring your equality jabber here, lady, you name one six-foot woman in town, and I'll eat my broom."

Now, that would be a feat to witness. "I guess." But I'd seen enough things in my career to warrant the belief that anything was possible.

"I gotta get going," Ray said. "My eggs are probably ice cold by now. And that dumb cat is trying to drink your coffee, by the way."

"Shoot!" I spun around and groaned.

Curly Fries had managed to ram her face into the mug. By the time I'd wrested her free and washed off her whiskers, it was past 8:00 a.m., time for breakfast and a shopping spree.

I'd never had the opportunity to shop for dresses in Boston. I should've been excited for it, but I was too preoccupied by the puzzle and my nerves for the charity ball that evening.

Hopefully, Paul's sister would make it easy and be ridiculously tall.

"I feel like a pig in silk." Griselda ran her fingers down the length of the cocktail dress I'd picked out for her.

"You're in silk," I said. "But you're certainly not a pig." Grizzy was skinnier than me, but she was one of those women who'd always had low self-esteem when it came to her weight. Her mother had been model.

I sat at the table on the edge of the dance floor and people-watched at my leisure. Folks in tuxedos, ball gowns, cocktail dresses, swept around the dance floor in time to a waltz.

There were plenty of slow songs, but the overly-enthusiastic DJ in the corner had already played pop songs that had perplexed the older folks.

"This is... nice," Grizzy said.

"You don't sound so sure." I didn't stop scanning the attendees of the event.

The DJ scratched the track and switched it over to "Drop It Like It's Hot" by Snoop Dogg. The tick-tock of the song induced a mass exodus of seniors from the dance floor, and left a couple young adults jiving around in their place.

"Check it out." Grizzy pointed to the DJ booth.

A middle-aged woman with a sharp nose, spindly legs, and a mauve velvet dress that clung to her bones stood in front of the DJ, gesticulating wildly.

The DJ whipped off his lumo green headphones and gave the woman two thumbs up, oblivious to her displeasure.

"Who is that?" I asked.

"The DJ? I don't know. Some dude from the big city, I guess. They must've brought him in. Seems like they're having second thoughts now."

"No, the woman. Skin-and-bones lady. Who's she?"

"That's Frances Sarah." Grizzy gave me the side eye. "She's the one hosting the ball."

"Paul's sister."

"Don't get any smart ideas, Chris. You stay right here with me," Grizzy replied, and patted my arm.

Another man approached the ongoing argument. He was tall, with chin-length hair, messy. Reminded me of Aragorn from the *Lord of the Rings* I'd binge watched. I spent most nights reading fantasy back home, in Boston. It was a great escape from the reality of crime.

Mr. Aragorn tapped Frances Sarah on the shoulder. She rolled her eyes at him with so much meaning they should've fallen out of her

head, then continued berating Over Enthusi-
astic DJ.

"And the man?" I asked. "Who's that guy?"

"This is why you should've stuck around for the last twelve years," Griselda said. "If you had, I wouldn't be your people tour guide. And on your right, you'll see an exceptionally bored Griselda trying to work out what she'd like from the buffet table."

"Don't worry, it won't be for long. The minute I'm off sabbatical I'll be out of your hair and back in Boston."

"Oh," Grizzy said. "OK."

I tore myself from the disagreement. "I—Griz, it's a vacation for me. You know that."

"No, I know," she said. "I know. Ha, I'm being silly. It's nice to have another human being in the house with me, you know? Great company."

"I agree. I enjoy staying with you," I said. "Besides, my whole sabbatical thing will end months from now. We've got plenty of time together." I didn't want to leave Grizzy behind—I missed having a friend like her—but that didn't change the fact that I had a job to get back to. A job I loved. Every time I caught a killer or solved a case, it brought me closer to letting go.

"Good evening." Man's voice, right in front of our table. I hadn't even seen him approach. Shoot, had I lost my touch?

Grizzy and I looked up.

Arthur Cotton had parted his hair in a style right out of the 20s. It would've been cute if it hadn't made me want to bust my dress laughing. And my dress wasn't tight—I'd opted for a loose shift, cut below the knee and cinched at the waist.

"Arthur." Grizzy's attitude did a three-sixty.

"Hello, Griselda. You look beautiful this evening. And you do too, Miss Watson."

"Christie or Chris. Every time you call me Miss Watson I sprout a gray hair."

Arthur wasn't quite sure how to react to

that. He turned to Griz instead. "Are you enjoying your evening?"

"So far, yes," she said.

Gosh, this was the most awkward conversation. These two liked each other so much they didn't know how to deal with it.

"Yes, it's pleasant," Arthur said.

Pleasant? It was as boring as a snail marathon. Apart from the argument that had finally dispersed—Frances Sarah strode back to the other side of the hall, tailed by the lanky guy.

"Hey, Arthur, would you keep my seat warm?" I asked. "I'm going to grab some drinks. Shirley Temples. How does that sound, Griz?"

My friend was laser-focused on the detective..

"I could get the drinks for you ladies." Arthur shifted to my side of the table.

"Please," I said. "It's the 21st century." Even if his hair was straight out of *the Great Gatsby*.

"Take a seat. Relax. You're tired from all that investigating. Be right back." I scooched out of my chair and meandered off, making out as if I didn't have a care in the world.

I'd already homed in on my target. Or targets. Frances Sarah and Mr. Aragorn had left the booth—the DJ had switched back to a more moderate song—and stood near the bar. Neither of them were happy.

I sat on a stool closest to their position and placed my silver clutch on the barbar toptop.

"This is not the time." Frances Sarah placed emphasis on the same syllables Paul had. She didn't move like a spider, though. Her gait was sinuous.

"Then when is the right time?" Mr. Aragorn asked. "We've been putting this off forever and I'm tired, so tired, of waiting for you to wake up and realize that what we've done together—"

"Together?" Frances asked. "Together. You've got to be kidding me."

"I was there too. I helped planned it, and if you think I'm going to let you leave with all the glory you've got another thing coming, *honey*."

"Perfidious wretch. You're nothing, Pete," Frances replied, and it came out as a hiss.

"Don't use that smart speak with me, woman."

Pete. Hadn't Missi said that Pete was Frances' husband? And what glory were they after? Glory wasn't a term I'd associate with murder, but anything was possible.

"We are at a charity ball, Peter. A charity ball!" she thundered.

"Don't cause a scene." Pete glanced back at the bar. I shifted my gaze over the dance floor to our table where Grizzy and Arthur sat side-by-side, staring off in alternate directions, both blushing. I sharpened my peripheral view of the two suspects.

"This isn't about us. It's about the people." Frances moderated her tone. "We can discuss our personal problems later. Right now, I need you to stay out of the way. I have to announce the raffle winner in fifteen minutes."

"*We* have to announce it."

"No. You stay here. Do what you do best." She flicked her fingers toward the bar. Frances click-clacked off in her high heels, and Pete glared after her, hatred burning from him. He could've lit all the candles in the world with that heat.

He didn't approach the bar. He looked at me one last time, then made for the exit.

I chewed my bottom lip. The one thing that'd struck me throughout the argument, apart from the glory comment, was Frances' lack of grief. Everyone handled death and sadness differently, but she hadn't mentioned it once.

Unless that was what they'd been referring to all along.

## ❧ 10 ❧

Jarvis dinged the bell in the Burger Bar, and I walked to the kitchen window, wielding my tray. The morning rush in the restaurant had helped take my mind off what I'd heard at the ball last night.

The rest of the evening had passed uneventfully, unless Grizzy and Arthur refusing to make eye contact counted as eventful.

I'd hoped to speak to Frances, but she'd disappeared after the raffle announcement, and Pete hadn't been easier to find. The only information I had was that they were unhappy with each other and marital problems didn't equal a murder motive.

Between the countless baskets of fries, Mexican Fiesta Burgers, and glasses of milkshake, I'd almost forgotten about the case.

The case that was not *my* case.

I retrieved another burger and fries, nestled on a red-checked napkin in a basket. "Thanks, Jarvis."

He gave me a thumbs up. He'd been quiet this morning too. Perhaps, it was because Missi had swept up to the window and flirted with him relentlessly, this morning. She was nearly 80-years-old, but insatiable when it came to the chef.

I took the food to a table and placed it in front of one of the regulars. It was the guy with the hand tattoo. "Here you go, George." I put up my brightest, best customer smile.

George grunted, picked up the burger and bit into it. A jalapeño slice dropped out of the bun and plopped into his basket.

"Anything else?" I asked.

A grunt again, to the negative this time. He was the least talkative twenty-something-year-old I'd ever met. Maybe he'd spent up all his energy on social media.

"Enjoy."

Missi and Virginia were in their booth against the wall and waved me over on my way back to the counter. They'd been in the bar since it'd opened at 8am—Grizzy believed there wasn't a clock on burger cravings—and summoned me fifty times since then.

"What can I get you ladies?" I pulled up in front of their table, tray wobbling on my palm.

"The dirt," Missi said.

"Stop." Virginia balanced her chin on her fist. "But yes, dear, we'd appreciate it if you could tell us about what happened at the ball last night."

"Wh—what?" They couldn't know about the fight between Pete and Frances, could they? No one was that nosy, even two old biddies who had thumbs in every pie.

"I told you she's slow for a detective," Missi said.

"It's rude to talk about people when they're standing right in front of you. Learn manners." Virginia sighed.

"I call a spade a spade, woman. You've known that about me since we were children. I'm too old to change now."

"There's a difference between being down-to-earth and plain rude. I think if you moderated your tone you might—"

"What about last night?" I cut them off—an argument could go on for hours with these two. It'd taken me less than a week to work that out.

*Focus, Christie.* My inner voice sounded like my mother and it had a sobering effect on me no matter the situation.

Missi tut-tutted. "Last night was the charity ball, yes?"

"Yeah, you were the one who told me about it," I said. "Shouldn't you know that?"

"Ah ha, another one who calls a spade a spade." Virginia grinned.

"There's no need to be rude." Missi pursed her lips.

"What do you want to know about the ball?"

Missi and Virginia shared a glance, sisterly secrets passing between them at a rate of twenty billion gossip parts per minute. "You haven't noticed?" Virginia asked.

"What?"

"Grizzy." Missi tipped her chin toward my friend standing behind the milkshake machine.

Griz had taken up residence there this morning and hadn't moved since, unless it was to refill napkin dispensers or ring up an order.

"She's not in her right mind, dear," Virginia said. "She's been acting strangely all morning and we wondered if it was because of the—oh, the—how do I put this?"

"The corpse in the yard," Missi suggested.

"The stabbing in the bushes? Mr. Dead in the Flowerbed."

"Stop." Virginia raised her palm. "You have no respect for the deceased."

"The deceased had no respect for anyone when he was alive," Missi said. "Why should I start respecting him when he called me an old spinster twenty times a week? Respect is earned, and he lost that opportunity with me."

I studied Grizzy, brow wrinkling. She *had* been quiet this morning, but I'd been so busy with the breakfast rush I'd barely noticed.

"I don't think it's about Mr. Dead in the Flowerbed." There was a certain ring to that.

"Paul," Virginia said. "His name was Paul."

"Right. Although, I know she's struggling to sleep. We both are." It was one thing to investigate murders off the clock, but when it happened in the back yard and there was nothing I could do to solve it...

"Then what's the problem?" Missi asked.

"I think it's that detective. Arthur Cotton." I kept my voice low. "He was at the ball last night and yeah, they sat at the table together, but it was so darn awkward I wanted to pluck my eyeballs out."

"Heavens to Murgatroyd," Virginia said.

"Here we go again." Missi rolled her eyes.

"What do you mean?"

"It's the same thing every month. Grizzy and Arthur get a little closer, they both freeze up, a period of abject awkwardity ensues and—"

"Awk-what?"

"It's a word!" Missi clicked her tongue. "Fine. A period of total awkwardness. Does that suit you? So, that awkwardness follows, they slowly start to mellow toward each other and get all sweet-eyed and honey-glazed, and then bam!" Missi slapped the table.

George dropped his burger at the table over.

"Bam?"

"They freeze up again," Missi replied. "The cycle continues. That's self-explanatory."

"You're not great at storytelling," Virginia said.

"Says the queen of redundancy."

"Ladies, please." I patted the air. "Grizzy will figure something's up if we make too much fuss. I'll talk to her about it, all right?"

"You've got a lot of experience in love, then?" Missi looked me up and down. It was the doubtful gaze of a woman who'd seen people from all walks of life. "Really? You're all split ends and chewed up nails."

"She's got a lovely face and figure, though," Virginia put in.

"But she's not taking care of herself. I'd bet anything it's been years since she's been near a man in a romantic fashion. Let alone in a relationship with one." Missi wasn't wrong. I hadn't dated since I'd first arrived in Boston and that had ended horribly. My partner had left me for another woman. My literal partner, as in police partner and boyfriend.

"Oh, I bet she's seen her fair share of action. In relationships. Not that she's loose."

I wasn't much of a blusher but this conversation pushed me to the limits. Another customer entered the Burger Bar, granting me a reprieve.

Pete, Frances Sarah's husband, strolled up to the front counter. "Double Thick Chocolate Malt Milkshake to go," he said. No "please" or "thank you."

Grizzy gave him a wan smile and set to work on the order.

Pete. Fancy him promenading back into my mind. He was tall, too. But was he tall enough to match Ray's description from the night of Loopy Paul's murder? What had Frances and Pete meant last night—all that talk about planning and glory. Could it be that they'd murdered Frances' brother for money? Or even, power?

No, no, ridiculous. I didn't know enough about either of them to make that judgment and I certainly didn't have evidence to—

"Strange," Virginia said.

"What is?" I asked.

"It's Pete. He usually sits down for a burger and shake at this time. I wonder why he needs takeout."

"Maybe he's got somewhere to be," Missi said.

My curiosity had reached peak levels. I had to talk to Pete about what I'd witnessed last night or about his deceased brother-in-law.

"Make it snappy," Pete said, and clicked his fingers at Griselda. "I've got an appointment to get to."

"What appointment?" Missi whispered.

I stripped off my apron.

It was time for my mid-morning break. And a little mid-morning sleuthing.

ᴥ  11  ᴥ

Whatever it was, the man was up to no good. He hunched his shoulders and darted glances left and right as he weaved around corners and down side streets, nearing the suburbs of Sleepy Creek.

I kept my head down, following him, with my phone out as if I'd stumbled upon one of those viral articles, *10 Ways Your Cat Is Killing You*. He greeted people he passed, avoided dogs on the ends of leads and maintained a brisk pace.

Griselda had barely registered my request for time off. I'd have to give her the ol' flashlight in the eyes routine when I got home. Get to the bottom of her issues with Arthur.

Pete Dawkins took a left onto Old Dirt Road.

It was a literal dirt road, but no one in Sleepy Creek had renamed it. As kids, Grizzy and I had camped out in the woods around here and harassed the log cabin neighbors with our girly midnight squeals after ghost stories by the campfire.

Pete took one of the trails that led deeper into the woods.

"That's not creepy." I followed him, anyway. What important meeting did Pete have in the woods?

I tucked my cell phone into the front pocket of my jeans and braced myself against a tree, peeking around its trunk.

Pete walked toward a cabin at the path's end. I couldn't follow him without getting caught, so I slipped between the trees, wincing each time my clumsy feet snapped a twig or rustled a leaf.

Sweat trickled down the back of my neck.

The captain had told me I had the self-control of a chipmunk locked in a room full of nuts, and he wasn't wrong. I had discipline when it came to a case, but when it came to a lead, I couldn't help myself.

Pete Dawkins trooped up the stairs of the cabin, and I stalled, watching, waiting. He opened the front door, it creaked, and he entered, then banged it shut.

An old Ford truck, blue with rust around the edges of its doors, was parked in front of the house, and a flashy Chevrolet Suburban sat next to it. Sheesh, who was he meeting with? The mafia?

I crouched and darted from my cover, up to the side of the house. I kept low, listening hard, and circled the house slowly.

Voices drifted from a window near the back.

"You're late," a man said. Not Pete. This one had a gravelly voice, too many cigarettes.

Pete grunted. "You work for me. I can't be late."

"I won't be working for you much longer at this rate, Pete." The second guy's voice softened. "I know times are tough, buddy, but I'm not into pro bono work?"

A lawyer. But why did Pete need a lawyer? I scanned my surroundings. Anyone could be watching from the tree-line, yet I couldn't do much to hide myself.

"I'm not asking you to do this for free," Pete said, at last. "Do you want a drink? A glass of water, coffee or somethin'?"

"No. Let's get down to business."

"Fine," Pete said. "Fine by me, Sawyer. I want to get this over with. The sooner that uppity, mean—"

"Let's not go down that road." Sawyer the lawyer, huh. Fancy that. "I know you're reluctant to sign the divorce papers but—"

"Reluctant? I don't want a divorce. I want

my piece of the meal ticket. She's all about money behind the scenes. Did you know that, Sawyer?" Pete said 'Sawyer' like the 'Soya' in Soya Sauce. "Frances acts high and mighty in front of everyone, but she's a miser. Why shouldn't I get my take? She doesn't want to be with me anymore, fine, but I'll be sure that I'm well fed for the rest of my life."

The lawyer sighed. "If I'm going to represent you in proceedings I need to know what you want out of the divorce."

"I want money," Pete said. "And I want to keep the cabin. She's had me staying here for weeks. Dumped her darn brother on me too."

"Money and the cabin," Sawyer replied, and hummed under his breath—taking notes? "Anything else you'd like to discuss with Mrs. Dawkins and her lawyer?"

"She's not Mrs. Dawkins anymore. Or she won't be once these papers are signed. I— man, how did this happen? How did it fall apart?" He choked up.

"I'm sorry Pete. I don't know what to say."

Apparently, Sawyer hadn't been trained for this in law school. Go figure.

"It was that brother of hers. We never got a moment's peace. He was always coming around and complaining. And then a couple weeks ago he—"

The crunch of tires on dirt distracted me from my eavesdropping. I froze.

A car approached the parking area, and here I was surrounded by open space and the certainty of discovery. That would mean a call to the local police, and then to the ones in Boston and the captain himself.

I crouched-ran down the side of the cabin, the back of my neck prickling. A car door slammed. Footsteps advanced. I should've been too far for them to have seen me but I wasn't willing to take that chance.

I reached the corner, rounded it, and used the back porch for cover.

Noises sounded in the house. I peeked back and the right headlight of a sports car looked right back at me. I squirmed my cell phone out of my pocket. I had ten minutes to get back to the Burger Bar before Grizzy got suspicious. She might be distracted but she'd reprimand me if she suspected I'd decided to investigate Paul's murder.

A bang sounded close to the back porch.

"Don't you walk away from me, Pete," a woman said. "Don't you dare."

The lawyer's gravelly tones interjected. "Frances, I don't think now is a good time to talk about—"

The back door slapped open, and I almost lost bladder control. A hysterical laugh built in my belly. I'd run right into the new hotspot of activity.

*Run back down the side of the house.*

I slapped my back against the porch wall and sank low, just as footsteps clunked onto the wooden boards above my head. Worst stakeout *ever*.

"I don't want to speak to her. Get her out of here," Pete said.

I inched along the side of the house.

Likely, they wouldn't notice me even if I threw a Mardi Gras themed party on the lawn—they were too involved in their own drama—but I wasn't taking any risks.

"You have to talk to me, Pete. We have to talk about what happened," Frances said, in practiced snootiness. I'd been ready to give her the benefit of the doubt about the whole money thing until she'd arrived in a sports car.

"Nothing happened. Nothing." Which meant, of course, something *had* happened.

"Paul—"

"Leave him out of this," Pete said. "You have no respect for the dead."

"You want to talk about respect? You didn't even like the guy and now you want to take a piece out of his will? A bit of the pie for Pete, right? You're such a low life. You don't deserve anything from me or from him," Frances said.

"You were the one who wanted a divorce! And I cared for Paul when you wouldn't. He needed help, and I gave it to him. You ignored us both."

"You used Paul to get to me," Frances said. "You didn't care about him. You only had him at the cabin on the off chance that I might visit you."

"Please, you both have to calm down," Sawyer said, but even he sounded hot under the collar. This fondue pot was about to bubble over.

"Get out of here," Pete said. "You wouldn't talk to me at the event the other night, so now you'll talk to my lawyer. And I'll get what I want, Frances. You mark my words. I will get what is rightfully mine."

This was my chance. Frances would march round the corner to get back to her car in a second. I pushed off and sprinted toward the far end of the house. I squeezed between the suburban and the cherry red speedster and hauled butt down the dirt path.

The fight continued behind me, voices raised against each other.

I hit the woods and didn't stop until I'd reached Old Dirt Road, lungs burning. The pain was worth it. I had a suspect list.

But I was already late for work, and Grizzy would have questions.

❧   12   ❧

That evening Griz and I sat at her kitchen table feasting on another of her creations. She could pretend she didn't know how to cook all she wanted but the proof was in the pudding, or in this case, the cheesy quesadillas.

"What's up?" I asked. "You've been quiet all day."

Grizzy shrugged and took another bite of her food.

"Griz, I know you. We've chatted every

week for years since I left, and you've always told me what's on your mind," I said. Apart from the whole Arthur Cotton crush and the loneliness, of course. Grizzy liked to put up a brave face.

I let my quesadilla hover in mid-air. "Is it about Arthur?"

"What? No! Why would you even ask that?" Grizzy dropped her hands into her lap and wiped them on her napkin. "You'll think I'm overreacting, and I don't want to worry you."

"Worry me? Well, you've succeeded in making that happen."

Grizzy heaved a sigh. "It's not about Arthur. Well, it is but it isn't."

"Care to elaborate?"

"It's about the interview down at the station the other day," Grizzy said. "Things got weird, Chris. It made me uncomfortable."

"In what way?" My pulse skipped up a notch.

"I don't know. I guess it was the questions they were asking. How they phrased things. Arthur wasn't the one who talked to me either, it was Detective Balle, and he came down tough. I got the feeling he thinks I did it."

"No way. That's ridiculous. You're not capable of hurting anyone and if that was the case, why don't they investigate me?" I asked. "Or question me again?"

Grizzy worried her bottom lip with her teeth. "You might know I'm not capable, but the detectives have to investigate, right? And they're definitely investigating me."

"Yeah, but that doesn't explain why they wouldn't interview me, as well. I was the one who was with you when it happened," I said.

If the cops were serious about Griselda as a suspect they would've spoken to me first. I'd provided her 'alibi.'

"Maybe they're still piecing things together. Or they're going to interview you next.

Either way, it's freaking me out. I'm not used to this kind of attention." She swallowed. "I've noticed people staring at me in the bar. Every time I make a milkshake for a customer I swear they're... glaring. Missi, Virginia, George, everybody."

" "The interview is bothering you and it's changed your perspective of everything. I guarantee you Missi and Virginia don't think you did it. They're concerned about you because they noticed you're acting different."

"Really?"

"Yeah, they asked me about you." I left out the part about Arthur. "People are worried, that's all. I think it's because Sleepy Creek is so set in its ways. When anything changes it's the talk of the town."

"That's true," Grizzy said, and perked up a bit. "They still haven't stopped talking about your arrival."

"See? Wait, what?" I laughed. "What exactly are they saying?"

"Nothing specific. Questions about, you know, the past."

"Oh." I blew past that. Discussing what'd happened to my mother didn't rank high on the dinner table topic list.

"Yeah." Grizzy drank her soda, ice cubes clinking against the glass, and didn't add anything to the statement. I silently blessed her for it.

I searched for a change of topic and landed on the one thing that'd anger my friend rather than placate her. But I had to tell her now. Griselda worrying over her fate removed the option for secrecy.

"I've been checking out leads in the case," I said.

"What?"

I winced. Boy, this ought to be good.

Grizzy spluttered.

"You're turning red," I said. "Calm down."

"Calm down? You're—"

Curly Fries chose that moment to wander into the kitchen in search of quesadilla morsels. She sat beside Griselda's chair and *prrt-meowed*.

Griselda ignored her—miracles *did* happen—and continued the soundless gabbing like a fish out of water.

"I just followed leads, you know? Nothing serious."

"It *is* serious. You're going to lose your job if anyone finds out you're interfering in an investigation. Christie, you could land in jail. You *know* that. You of all people have to know that because you're a detective." Grizzy ripped up her napkin into tiny shreds.

"I do know that, but it's my choice to make," I said.

"Fine, it's your choice." She threw her hands up and specks of napkin fluttered to the tiles. One landed on Curly Fries' nose, and the cat pawed it off and meowed again.

"I don't want to feel guilty about this, and I know that I should leave it up to Detective Balle, but you don't understand what this is like for me."

"Help me understand," Grizzy replied.

"It's like, uh, how do I put this?" I glanced out of the kitchen window. Shades of gray played over the porch, and the cordoned off back garden. The police line against the fence vibrated, shaken by the breeze. "It's Sleepy Creek and it's a case. I know it's not my case and that it's a threat to everything, but every time I think about it I think about —*her.* I think about what she'd do in the situation."

"She wouldn't endanger her future," Griselda said.

"She'd investigate. She was driven."

Grizzy's lips grew thin and tight. She had an opinion and didn't want to share it.

"Say it," I said.

"Don't take this the wrong way but your mother isn't the best example, Chris. She went too far a lot of the time. You remember the trouble she got into investigating her cases. You remember what it was like because you lived it."

"Things changed when we came to Sleepy Creek," I said.

"Your mother hated Sleepy Creek."

"You're right there." I sighed. "I don't know what's wrong with me. I've got a burning desire to find the truth. About everything. About every case and especially hers, but I'm too scared to touch that one so…"

Grizzy got up and fetched kibble for Curly Fries. She poured it into the bowl and the rattle filled the silence. Curly Fries sniffed the food, turned up her nose, and stalked out of the kitchen again.

"I don't want you to get in trouble," Grizzy said. "But if you need to do this I won't stop you. Not that I can, ha. You're the most stubborn person I've met. Just don't do anything crazy, OK? No snooping around and making people angry. Nothing illegal."

"Of course," I said. Stubborn was good in my books—it meant I kept at it until I found the answers I needed.

A knock sounded at the front door, and we

both hopped on the spot. The clock read 7:30pm. "Expecting visitors?" I asked.

Grizzy led the way through the living room to the front door. The knock didn't let up. "Who's there?" she called out.

"It's Detective Balle. Open up, Miss Lewis."

Grizzy let the detective into the living area, casting furtive looks in my direction as if I'd know what this was about. Technically, we both knew what this was about. Balle might've come because he'd discovered my forest-spelunking shenanigans from the afternoon.

"Detective Balle," Grizzy said, "how are you this evening?" She placed emphasis on the last word.

"Sorry to interrupt you at this time of the night," Balle said, "but crucial evidence has emerged and I need to talk to you about it."

"Of course," Griselda replied. "Let me clear dinner off the table."

Balle coughed. "It's Miss Watson I need to talk to."

The air went out of the room. Grizzy and I floundered for words. The question I'd asked earlier slammed home.

*Surely, the detective would have spoken to me if he'd had suspicions about Griselda?*

Oh, boy. "Sure." I gestured to the sofas directed at the flat screen TV in Grizzy's entertainment center. "We can all talk in the living room."

"I need to speak to you, ma'am. In private. This interview is better conducted at the station."

"There's no need for that." If he imagined I'd go down to the station at this hour, willingly, he had another thing coming. I'd lawyer up so fast his world would invert, right itself, and then spin off its axes. The advantages of knowing my rights after reading them to others countless times. "Anything you need to speak to me about, Griselda can hear too. We're living together and we witnessed the crime together."

Fat chance he'd let that one slide. Balle directed that piercing too-handsome scowl at me. "This is *my* investigation, Watson, not yours. You will proceed accordingly."

He was within the bounds of the law to ask me to speak with him privately. I could refuse, sure, but he'd get a warrant, and I'd find out nothing about the case in the interim. I needed Balle to remain open to prompting here.

"All right," I said. "I'll make us a cup of coffee before we start."

Griselda processed the interaction in a series of head positions, first to me then back to Balle, then to me again. Finally, she made a tiny grunt and trooped toward the staircase.

I whipped up the pot of coffee, a tray of mugs, sugar, cream, everything Balle might need to loosen the tongue, then carried it through to the living room where he sat in one of the armchairs. He was out of place between the flower vase and the book case in the corner. He shifted in his seat as if aware of that.

"It's good." I positioned the tray on the coffee table. "Griselda has excellent taste in coffee."

Detective Balle took a cup and dumped three sugars into it. He stirred and plinked the spoon against the rim.

"That's a lot of sugar," I said.

"I need it. Sweetens up my sour attitude." Balle flashed me a grin. A brief show of the man rather than the detective.

I couldn't allow myself to forget that he was a detective, though. "What do you need to talk to me about?"

Balle withdrew two items from his breast pocket—a notepad and a plastic bag containing a slip of white paper. "As I said, new evidence has come to light. It involves you, directly."

"What? That's impossible."

Balle hesitated. "I—uh. I want to make this as painless and professional as possible."

"OK?"

"I understand that you've had a turbulent history with Sleepy Creek," Liam continued, and my throat closed a little—how much did this detective know about me? He hadn't been around when Griz and I had attended high school.

Balle waited for me to say something. If he already knew, I didn't need to fill him in on the details. If he didn't, I'd prefer it stayed that way. I wasn't ashamed of my mother, but the pain was there. The only person who I talked with about it was Griselda, and even we avoided the topic as a general rule.

"I'm not here to mince words." Balle did precisely that.

"Then don't. Get to the point. I appreciate expediency, it's part of the job description."

Balle rolled the pads of his thumbs against each other. "We found a torn picture on Paul's person. It took us time to identify it and cover our bases."

"All right."

He held out the plastic bag that contained that slip of paper. His fingertips brushed mine and sent a jolt through me.

I snapped my hand back, taking the evidence bag, and sucked in a breath. Why was I so nervous? It was a picture. But who was in it? Or what?

I turned the bag over. The coffee table swam beyond the center point of my focus. It was my mother—torn around the edges but smiling up at me, the sun forming a halo around her dark locks.

I didn't want to show weakness in front of Balle, but this was the first time I'd seen her face in ten years. I'd hidden the pictures I'd had of her after a night of wine and weeping in my student apartment back before I'd become an officer.

"Do you need a minute?" Liam asked.

"No." I tore myself from the image. "Why did Loo—Paul have this?"

"I hoped you'd be able to shed light on that," Balle said.

"Me?"

"Yes. You understand how this appears, right?"

I didn't want to admit I did.

"Your mother's case was never solved. You left town years ago, according to my reports, and the day you return a man with your mother's picture is murdered in your best friend's back yard?"

"You think I did it," I said, and snorted, because it was ridiculous. I was a homicide detective. What, did he think I'd gone all *Dexter* on Paul and lost it because of a sabbatical?

"I don't think anything. I follow the leads," Liam replied.

"I don't know why Paul had a picture of my mother. I got rid of all that stuff years ago and anything we had left over was placed in storage. The house was, well, you know what happened to it, I'll wager. It was razed to the ground." All the evidence destroyed.

"Which means Paul must've had this image for quite some time. Do you know if he was involved with your mother?"

"No! No, I mean, I didn't even know Paul existed until a few days ago," I said. "And I have no idea why he would have the picture or why he would've climbed over our back fence."

"Perhaps, he wanted to talk to you."

"About my mother? I didn't even know the guy." Despite what Grizzy might think, I hadn't come back to Sleepy Creek to investigate my mother's death. I'd come back to prove that I could move on. That it was in the past and it wasn't the reason I'd gone on a tangent in my last case.

But this changed everything. A picture of my mother on the body of a murder victim. How was she involved? Why?

I couldn't tell Liam I'd done investigating

of my own without landing in trouble with him and my captain back in Boston.

"You can't think of any reason why Paul would've had this image?"

"No, I can't. I could make deductions from a professional standpoint but not a personal one."

"Thank you for your time, Miss Watson," he said, and laid out his palm.

I didn't give him the picture back. I studied her expression, the joy, the sweet smile.

"Miss Watson? I'm going to need that picture—"

I placed it in his hand and turned my head.

Liam Balle rose from the armchair and towered over me, his woody cologne light on the air. "I'll be in touch," he said, softly. He left the living room and let himself out—the only indication he'd left was the click of the front door.

I stared at the tray on the table and Balle's

half-empty mug. My mother. How was she in-volved in this?

"Chris?"

Grizzy hovered beneath the arch that led into the kitchen.

"Hey," I said.

"Gosh, what happened? What did he say? You look like you've seen a ghost."

That was because I had.

❧ 14 ❧

I put the tray on the counter in the Burger Bar and tapped my heel in time to the upbeat pop song that jammed through the speakers overhead, low enough to encourage conversation but loud enough to be enjoyed. I had to act natural.

Griselda had been wrinkling her brow at me and pouting all morning. I'd told her what'd happened with the detective the night before and extricated myself from her probing questions before midnight.

"Order up," Grizzy said, and placed the

Double Thick Chocolate Malt Milkshake on the tray. "How are you feeling?"

I whisked the shake off the counter without replying. I was fine. I was a little freaked about the picture, but I hadn't had *the* nightmare last night. I'd expected it after seeing her face again.

Whenever I went through a rough patch, *that* nightmare would crop up again. The darkness, smoke, the house burning, and sirens wailing. And I'd be there, eighteen-years-old and unable to help. They'd hold me back, and I'd scream for her, over and over again.

"She's dawdling past our table," a voice said, loudly. "This new girl needs work."

Missi's glare cut right through my melancholy. I backpedaled and placed the shake in front of her. "And good morning to you too, Mississippi."

"Oh, you've got a smart mouth on you," she said, and stripped the paper off her straw. She hated it when people called her by her full name.

"How are you this morning, dear?" Virginia asked. "Griselda tells us you had a bit of a scare last night?"

"No scare," I replied. "I'm fine."

"Ah the mantra of the clinically insane," Missi said, between moist slurps. "Or was that the clinically depressed?"

"Somebody didn't get her sugar rush this morning." I winked at her. It'd been a week, but we'd already fallen into a comfortable routine of teasing each other.

"Well, you've been wandering around with that long face, it's no wonder I'm cranky."

"Rein it in, dear." Virginia patted the table. She never lost her temper, but I didn't want to be around the day she did. She seemed like the type who bottled it up for years until she exploded.

"Nice chat," I said, and checked the clock. I had a short break coming up when Martin, Grizzy's manager, arrived. "But I've got to get back to work. Do you ladies need anything else?"

"No thank you, dear," Virginia said.

I swept off to the next table, and the next, taking orders and delivering them to Jarvis. Each Mexican Fiesta Burger received a shake of the maracas and extra jalapeños. People loved them. They couldn't get enough of the spicy tang, the juicy patty and the melty cheese.

My mouth was a water fountain at work thanks to the smells and sights. Jarvis outdid himself every time.

At 10:00 a.m., Martin entered the restaurant. Short but handsome, dark skin, neat uniform with the Burger Bar logo, ironed, not a crease in sight. He took pride in his work.

"Morning," he said, and grinned at me. "How are you today?"

"Great," I said. "In need of a break." He didn't look a lot like Jarvis, and he didn't speak like him either. Martin's parents were from New York, but his grandparents lived in Jamaica.

"Take it." Martin grinned, slipping on his apron.

I stripped off mine then dumped my tray next to the mixer.

"Break?" Griselda asked.

"Yeah." I handed her my apron. "I'm going to catch some fresh air. Maybe get a coffee from the café down the street."

"We've got a coffee machine."

"Fresh air." I smiled at her.

Grizzy's expression crumpled from concern to suspicion. "Christie—"

"Be back later." I waved and made a beeline for the exit. So, I wasn't the best actress in the world. I'd spent all morning turning the evidence and facts over and reached a conclusion.

I had to get back to Pete's house and find out if he had anything that connected him to my mother. Paul had stayed in his house before he'd been killed. That made Pete suspect number one, and the fact that he wanted money didn't better my opinion of him.

I passed the morning shoppers and folks like me who'd caught a quick break from work. I waved at the florist, Nelly Boggs, and she grinned back at me and pushed her glasses up her nose, fingers hidden by a fuzzy sweater.

Only a week and the folks I remembered from high school, the ones who hadn't left Sleepy Creek, greeted me like I'd never left. It gave me a warm, cozy feeling inside that was unfamiliar.

Small town living had its ups and downs. Warmth versus gossip and, now, murder. I took a left then a right, working out the quickest route to Pete's cabin in the woods. I reached Old Dirt Road fifteen minutes later.

I'd made good time, considering Griselda would expect me back by 11:00 a.m. at the latest. I took the path through the woods and hovered behind the trees, spying on Pete's place between the branches.

The patch of grass in front of the cabin was empty of cars. A good sign.

"Take it easy," I said.

A twig cracked behind me, and I spun around, heart pounding. Nothing but woodland greeted me. The wind whispering through the long blades of grass. Nothing made me jumpier than the prospect of finding evidence that related to my mother's murder.

I 'womanned up' and slipped out of the woods, hurrying across the lawn toward the front steps. I took them two at a time, then came up short. The front door was locked, and I wasn't about to break, enter and leave a trail behind.

Pete struck me as the type of guy who kept a spare set of keys hidden somewhere.

His worn welcome mat yielded nothing but dust and a sneeze, and there wasn't anything atop the lantern fixed to the wall either.

"Shoot." I couldn't turn back now. I'd already committed to this as much as it was possible to commit to an illegal investigation.

I vaulted the balustrade and landed in the dirt because why not pull out the cop moves? I needed to stretch those muscles or they'd atrophy, and I'd be the laughing stock back in Boston.

I circled the house to the back porch.

"What?" I whispered. "No way."

The back door's jamb had splintered, and cold wind rattled through the gap. Pete must've broken it during his argument with Frances Sarah.

I tried the back door and suppressed a rush of triumph when it opened.

The dingy kitchen had no stove, but a microwave in the corner and a bar fridge beside it. I walked around the kitchen table, wood stained by heaven alone knew what, and into the living area.

"Rooms, Chris, find the rooms," I muttered.

The cabin wasn't exactly the Ritz. I didn't have too many directions to go in. The first room was a bathroom, faucet dripping in the sink, the next one a well-lit bedroom, queen-sized bed unmade, and the third...

"Jackpot." I entered the gloomy room with

the single bed and twitched the curtains apart, allowing a sliver of light through the dusty pane.

This *had* to have been Loopy Paul's bedroom while he'd stayed with Pete. A desk in the corner stoked my intrigue. I strode to it, checked the time and almost had a heart attack—Griselda would expect me back in twenty minutes—then rifled through the drawers.

The top and middle yielded nothing. I clunked open the bottom one and felt the wooden base. It rattled. Loose? Could this be a secret compartment? I pinched my fingers around the edges of the base and caught the corner. I lifted a length of thin plywood. It was a false bottom.

I felt underneath the plywood and drew out a letter, yellowed with age. "Please be relevant," I whispered. I let the plywood scrape back into place, then backed away from the desk to read by the window.

*Dear Paul,*

*I understand you're concerned for my safety but there's not much I can do right now. I've always appreciated your help but I have to deal with this on my own.*

*Let me be clear, it wouldn't be appropriate for you to get involved, no matter how much you want to help. My cases are my responsibility.*

*I hope you and your sister are well.*

*Warmest Regards,*

*Detective Watson*

It was from my mother. I massaged my chest, right over my heart, and exhaled.

My mother had been friends with Paul. I'd never seen him at our house in my entire life. Not once. Unless he'd been a colleague? She'd never mixed work with home life and she hadn't spoken about her investigations before or after we'd arrived in Sleepy Creek.

If her murder had been linked to an old case, and Paul's murder was linked to hers then—

"Are you crazy?" a woman asked.

I jumped and threw the letter into the air.

Grizzy stared at me from the bedroom door, arms folded. It was as if I'd teleported back to the Burger Bar. "Have you lost your mind?"

"What are you doing here?" I hissed, and snatched the letter from the floor. I folded the page and tucked it into my back pocket, palms slippery with sweat. "Did you follow me here?"

"Heck yes, I followed you here. I knew you were going to do something stupid, Chris, but this? Breaking and entering? Are you trying to get yourself fired? Are you—?"

A car engine growled outside, and we both froze. Doors slammed. Voices rose and carried through the tiny house. Nowhere to run or hide. Not even a closet.

"Hurry!" I wormed my fingers under the bottom rail of the window and forced it up. I winced at the scrape of wood on wood, then leaped out of the opening and rolled onto the grass outside.

I ran a few paces, crouched over, then turned back to watch for my friend.

Except she wasn't inbound. She was stuck, the top strap of her apron hooked on the window latch.

"Grizzy!" I ran back for her.

She shook her head.

"What the heck?!" Someone yelled inside the house.

"Go," Griselda grunted. "Just leave."

I didn't have a choice.

## ❦ 15 ❦

I paced back and forth in front of the reception desk at the police station, sneakers squeaking on the linoleum. "How much longer is this going to take?" I asked. "I've done everything by the book. Paid the bail and—"

"She's being processed," the receptionist said, in a nasal whine. She pushed horn-rimmed glasses up the bridge of her nose. "It won't be much longer now. Please take a seat." She sounded perpetually bored.

"Listen, Glenda, I'm a detective myself and—"

"I wouldn't throw that around in here, Watson. It doesn't hold much weight, right now." Detective Balle strode out of his office, the top button of his shirt undone. Messy. Very unlike him. He was stressed out, and I had a hunch why that might be.

"Detective," I said.

"Miss Watson. Care to explain how your best friend wound up in a current suspect's house, hanging from one of the window latches?"

"Are you trying to be funny?"

"No."

"Good, because it's not working." I was in terrible mood. Between the letter I'd found and Grizzy's arrest, I didn't need the added pressure. This was my fault. When the residents of Sleepy Creek found out Griselda, the sweetheart of the town, had been arrested they'd want to blame someone for it.

Naturally, that someone would be me. And

they wouldn't be wrong about that. If I'd kept my nose out of police business this would never have happened. But my mother was involved. My mother!

Balle folded his arms and bore down on me, using all six somethin' of those feet to make his presence known. "What did you do, Watson?"

"Nothing," I said. "I did nothing except bail my friend out of a tight spot."

"You expect me to believe this is a coincidence? That your friend happened to be in Pete's house, in Paul's old bedroom, and—"

"She was in Paul's bedroom?"

"Don't play dumb, Miss Watson."

Glenda sniffed and crinkled the pages of her lifestyle magazine.

"Who do you think you're talking to like that?" I asked. "Didn't your mother teach you any manners?"

Liam deflated somewhat. "I—uh, sorry. Sorry. I'm frustrated. This is the first murder we've had in Sleepy Creek in years. We don't have much by way of a homicide department, of course. We handle everything from murder to theft around here."

"Who was the last murder?"

"It was a case of self-defense. Two fishermen got into a fight and—listen, that's not the point. I need an assurance from you that you're not trying to investigate this case. I don't need a big city cop barging in with high and mighty intentions of solving the crime."

"I'm not doing anything like that." But only because I wasn't technically a detective while I was on sabbatical.

"Why don't I believe you?"

I wriggled my nose from left to right. "Look, how much longer is this going to take? I need to get Grizzy home."

"She'll be out in a second." Liam didn't relax an iota. "You're lucky Pete decided not to press charges."

"I'm lucky?"

"Yes. You can bet that everyone in this

town would blame you if their favorite restaurateur wound up behind bars," Liam said.

"But I wasn't the one—"

He shrugged. "It wouldn't matter to them. There are already whispers about you around town."

"Mmhmm." That came from Glenda. I glared at her, and she lifted her magazine and hid behind Rihanna's face on the front cover.

"What whispers?" If folks around here suspected me of anything it wouldn't bode well for my best friend or her business.

"The kind I don't care to repeat," Balle said, and adjusted his belt. "Miss Watson, stay out of trouble."

"I'm not in trouble."

"Not yet." He sauntered off before I could reply, giving me a view of his broad back. That provided a brief distraction, but no relief from the churning in my stomach. What would Griselda say when she got out? Would she blame me for everything?

A commotion at the end of the hall drew me from those unsavory ruminations.

Grizzy had finally appeared and every ounce of guilt I'd held back slapped me in the face like a two week old trout.

Griselda carried her apron over her arm, neatly folded, of course, and readjusted her cardigan. Arthur Cotton came with her, pausing every other step to peer at her. They didn't talk.

Grizzy walked right past me and headed for the station's exit.

"Thank you." Glenda waved with her magazine. "Come again!"

"Glenda," Arthur said. "Get it together."

I ignored the peanut gallery and sprinted after my friend. I crashed out of the police station, but Griselda hadn't waited for me. She was already halfway down the street, headed in the direction of her house, and Grizzy didn't have a car.

I ran after her. "Wait! Griselda, wait."

She didn't. She raised her chin.

I caught up to her and grasped her forearm. "Grizzy, please. I'm so sorry."

She wrenched out of my grip. "No."

"What?"

She stopped and glared at me. "You don't get to say that."

"What? Why not?"

"Because you're not sorry. Don't lie to me, Christie. You'd sneak off and do the exact same thing again given half the chance. And don't tell me you're going to stop investigating this case because I know you won't." She trembled, strings of her blonde hair falling from her messy bun. "Don't lie to me anymore. I can't stop you from doing any of this and no, I won't kick you out of my house, but I need you to be honest with me."

"I have been—"

"Christie!"

"Fine" I slapped my hands against my thighs. "I was trying to protect you by keeping it a secret. But I told you I was checking it out. You said it was my choice."

"That's a load of hogwash," she replied. "You knew it would make me angry if you broke into someone's house, and that's why you kept this to yourself."

"You're making out like I'm super selfish. I did want to protect you, and yeah, I also didn't want to make you angry. Can't it be both those things? Grizzy, I hardly expected you to follow me to Pete's place."

"I had to catch you," she said. "I knew you wouldn't tell me anything real until I caught you red-handed. It wasn't my best idea, but I guess that's why we're friends. We're cut from the same cloth when it comes to dumb ideas."

We fell silent for a minute, but neither of us laughed at the lame joke. Grizzy started off again, and I matched her pace.

"I'll go to a motel," I said.

"Don't be ridiculous."

"You don't want to know about the case."

"I don't," Grizzy said. "But I do. I want to understand why you're doing this. I know your mom is involved, but I didn't expect you to go to these lengths. That was dangerous. I guarantee you Pete wouldn't have dropped the charges if he'd caught you. You're an outsider."

"I found something important." I filled her in on the letter between Paul and my mom.

Grizzy listened in silence. "I don't know what to tell you, Chris. I'm not going to report you to the cops if you continue investigating but I—I don't know what to do anymore. You're putting yourself in difficult situations."

"Just trust that I know what I'm doing."

Griselda sighed. "I think we should stop talking now," she said. "I need room to breathe. I've got a lot on my mind."

"I understand."

We walked home in silence, and when we got there Grizzy went straight to bed, Curly Fries in tow. I had to be the worst house guest Griselda had ever had. She'd expected us to have slumber parties, watch movies, and eat popcorn. Instead, I'd taken up a case that wasn't mine and endangered our friendship, and my future too.

I touched my back pocket and fingered the outline of the letter. I couldn't stop now. Not when I was this close to discovering the truth.

## ❧ 16 ❧

I lifted Grizzy's note off the kitchen table, and used my free hand to rub the sleep from my eyes. I gave the clock a bleary once over. It was 7:00 a.m., and I'd overslept. Last night's dreams had been more nightmares and they'd kept me in that horrible limbo state halfway between sleep and awake.

I squinted at Griselda's neat handwriting.

*Stay home today and get some rest. Martin is taking your shifts in the Burger Bar. G.*

That was it. The decision had been made for me. I wanted to believe Grizzy had my best interests at heart, but I was sure she needed space from me and my antics. I didn't blame her.

No doubt, the restaurant would be alive with gossip this morning, and I'd catch plenty of dirty stares if I turned up. Not that they scared me or anything, but that atmosphere wasn't optimal for a place like Grizzy's.

I sighed and crumpled up the note then dropped it into the trash can.

Curly Fries meowed and paced in front of her empty kibble bowl. I would've refilled it for her but she'd already crunched through an entire morning's worth of the stuff. She was a pig in cat's clothing.

I fixed a fresh pot of coffee, working everything over in my mind. I couldn't stay home all day—I'd lose my mind worrying about my mother's murder and the leads in the case. The letter. Paul must've known her well to have been concerned for her safety.

The same Loopy Paul who had clambered over the back fence with her picture tucked into his coat. Was it possible he'd been on his way to give me information about my mom's case? But that would mean whoever had killed him had a stake in it too.

I poured myself a cup of Joe, took a sip and winced. I'd forgotten the sugar. I spooned some in and stirred it, then tried again.

"Better," I murmured.

My mother was involved. I'd established that. It had clouded my vision, but there wasn't a chance on this good Earth that I would stop trying to figure out what had happened to her now that I'd taken up the mystery. I could head out and talk to Pete, but he hadn't seemed that stable both times I'd sneaked around his house unseen.

*Ha, look who's talking.*

And that left Paul's last blood relative. Frances Sarah. The charity queen herself, who drove a red sports car down a dirt road without any concern for the car's paint job or undercarriage. Sacrilege. Jeremy Clarkson was in tears somewhere.

If Paul had been close to my mother years ago, in his early twenties, it stood to reason that Frances Sarah might've been connected to her too. And that made her priority number one on my list.

I slapped back the rest of my coffee, spared a quick pat for pig-cat, then went up-stairs to change.

I researched Frances Sarah on my phone, and the address for her office at Sleepy Charity for Apnea Disorders, blinked at the entendre, then sprang to action.

Ten minutes later, I was ensconced in a cushy armchair that would've put an insom-niac to sleep, while the receptionist behind a matte-black desk droned into the office phone's receiver.

"Sleepy Charity for Apnea Disorders," she said. "Yes. No. Mrs. Dawkins is in a meeting, currently. Yes. And who may I say is calling?" She frowned and drew the phone from her ear. "Rude."

"Hang up on you?" I asked.

The receptionist, Megan, gave me a gaze as empty as the Grand Canyon. "Mrs. Dawkins will be with you presently."

Tough crowd. I twiddled my thumbs and checked the time on my leather-strapped watch every couple seconds. I needed to do *something,* even if it was as simple as lifting my wrist and glaring at it—it wasn't as if I had anywhere to be other than Grizzy's place, contemplating my poor life choices.

"Miss Watson?"

I jerked upright and came face-to-face with the spindly sister herself. "Hi," I said. "Call me Christie."

"Frances Sarah Dawkins," she said, and extended her hand.

Another shake—I'd been treated to plenty this week, if treat was the appropriate term for it. "It's nice to meet you, at last."

Frances Sarah wasn't as pleased to see me. "Megan tells me you have an important matter to discuss with me? About... about Paul."

"That's correct. I didn't want to alarm you,

but I didn't want my visit confused with any-thing, uh, sleep related."

"Let's talk in my office." Frances gestured to a misted glass door.

I followed her into a space organized to perfection. The desk pad was centered and a pen holder placed at an angle, a couple of inches from the corner of the desk. The effect was replicated by a miniature Zen sand garden and rake. I got the feeling Frances Sarah had used a ruler when organizing her setup.

"Please, take a seat."

I did as I was told and observed in silence, mentally cataloguing the oddities in Frances' office. An image of the Eiffel tower behind her petite leather chair. A potted cactus near the door. Cream drapes that obscured most of the light streaming through the window.

Everything about Frances Sarah was at odds with itself. She clicked across the hard-wood floor and took her position. She waited for me to talk, her forearms resting on the desk.

"Thank you for seeing me," I said.

"I'm not sure I can say it's a pleasure yet. The only people I've spoken to about Paul are the police."

Not technically true. She'd screamed about him over at Pete's place earlier in the week. At least, Balle had done his job properly and taken her statement. Or was he considering her as a suspect?

"I'm in a unique position," I said. "I've just come back to town, and the night I arrived, Paul was found in my best friend's back yard. And to make matters even stranger, and sadder, your brother was found with a picture on his person."

Frances perked up. "A picture?"

"Yeah. It was of my mother."

"Your mother?"

"That's correct. My mother was murdered twelve years ago." I swallowed. "And normally I don't discuss this kind of thing with anyone, but I figured if anyone would know why Paul had that picture it would be you."

Silence followed that statement.

"This is a discussion better left for law enforcement."

"I am law enforcement." I whipped that "card" out and instantly regretted it. *Christie, you're doing it again.* Anything to get answers. Anything to solve a case.

"You're a detective?"

"Yes," I said. "But not in Sleepy Creek. I'm from Boston." Balle would have kittens if he caught wind of this. No, he'd have Curly Fries. Millions of Curly Fries-sized cats with ugly, sharp faces. "I'm not technically investigating your brother's murder, but it directly involves me and my family and another murder that I am keenly interested in solving. Any information you could offer me would be greatly appreciated."

"Is it legal for us to have this discussion?" Frances asked. "I have a reputation to uphold."

And car repayments to make. "Let's put it this way, I'm only asking from a place of interest. Personal interest. If you refuse me the information there's nothing I can do, but please, I—this is my mother. It's—you understand what it's like to lose someone. It's—" I cut off. None of it was an act. I couldn't put this into words properly. I'd lost her years ago, but I had *never* let it go.

Frances didn't get up, but those sharp eyes flicked from side-to-side in their sockets. I was weighed and sorted. Catalogued, even. "All right," she said. "Who was your mother?"

Bingo. I was in. "Lillian Watson."

Frances paled.

"Are you all right?"

She exhaled. "Fine. Just that name brings back unpleasant memories from my childhood. Your mother was the officer who helped my brother and me relocate to Sleepy Creek years ago."

"She—what?" My mind was blown. If that was the case, it meant they'd—

"I was in my late twenties when it happened," she said. "Paul and I lived in Boston.

We got in trouble with a bad crowd. It was my fault. I fell in love with a man who wasn't good for either of us. Paul was out of work at the time, and Connor offered him a job. Before we knew it, we were in too deep. They asked Paul to do things he refused to do."

"Like what?"

Frances' jaw worked. "Illegal things."

"Was Connor part of an organized crime family?" I asked.

"Yes," Frances said, "and your mother busted Paul on the way back from a job. He became an informant, and she helped us extricate ourselves from the group. I don't know all the details, but I think she moved to Sleepy Creek to watch over us. Or it was because Connor found out about her helping us out."

My heart rate skyrocketed. This was news to me. "What happened to Connor and the family?"

"The Somerville Spiders," Frances said. "They were wiped out. Your mother helped bring the bosses to justice, as far as I know."

Then there had to be a lot of angry men in prison, itching to get rid of the woman who'd destroyed them. Could this be it? Could this be the link I'd searched for all along? But if that was the case, surely the detective on my mom's case would've investigated that avenue? I needed more information. Evidence. A lead.

"Paul wrote my mother a letter, and this was her reply," I said, and removed it from my pocket.

Frances took her time reading it. "I'm sorry," she said. "I have no idea what she's referring to here. After we came here, everything settled. Paul had nightmares and sleep apnea but that was about it."

"The letter refers to a case." A case my mother must've been investigating in this town itself. "Any idea what that was about?"

"None at all."

A dead end there, but I had one lead to follow. The Somerville Spiders.

"Can you tell me anything about your brother? Are there any enemies he might've had? Anyone who might've wanted to hurt him?"

Frances puffed out her cheeks. "Let's face it, Paul wasn't the easiest guy to get along with. He had his quirks."

Like a fiery hatred for jalapeños.

"But honestly, no. I don't think anyone would go so far as to do this. I—no. It's nothing."

"Nothing?"

"Well, I guess it might be something. Paul stayed with my ex-husband after we separated. He preferred Pete's company to mine, but Paul was a burden only family should carry."

A burden. That was a harsh way to talk about a relative.

"Paul blamed me for what happened in Boston. He believed that if I'd never gotten involved with Connor, he would never have been in the Somerville Spiders. We fought a lot because of it, and he had a myriad of ticks and disorders, as well. Needless to say, he was difficult to live with."

"So he stayed with Pete."

"Yes. About two weeks ago, Pete approached me about him. He told me that Paul had been behaving differently. Staying up late. Sneaking around." Frances lifted the mini-rake and dragged it through the sand of her Zen garden, leaving three shallow tracks. "Honestly, that's all I know. And I'm only telling you this because I understand that you've got a stake in what happens. I lost my brother, but I can't imagine what it must have been like to lose a parent."

I rose from my seat. "Thank you for speaking with me, Mrs. Dawkins."

Frances nodded. "Stay safe."

That sounded ominous rather than comforting.

"The Somerville Spiders," I muttered and strode down the sidewalk, past cute storefronts decorated with flowers for the upcoming spring festival. "Spiders." I had to find out more about them.

They were Boston-based but I'd never heard of them, which meant they'd been eradicated years ago or had dissolved and joined the other gangs now prevalent in the city. Mobsters were notoriously difficult to bust, and I'd always been glad that wasn't my job.

Only a handful of the murders that had crossed my desk had been linked back to one of the crime families, and those had led to swift arrests and convictions. The men had ended up in prison, the family had been untouched and had distanced themselves from their actions.

I turned the corner and continued down the road, traveling the circuit I'd chosen subconsciously.

If my mother had led to the Spiders' end, perhaps it was a Spider who had murdered her. But would a Spider stay around this many years to kill Paul? What if Paul's death wasn't linked to my mom's murder? What if it was a coincidence?

"No, no. Has to be linked. Has to be."

I stopped in front of Grizzy's Burger Bar and peeked through the front windows.

Virginia and Missi sat in their usual booth, drinking milkshakes and people-watching. Grizzy chatted with Martin across the counter, dark half-moons beneath her eyes.

A wave of guilt crashed over me.

I needed to apologize to Grizzy then go home and figure this out in silence. I'd flip open my laptop and research the Spiders to my heart's content.

*Come on, Chris. Get it together.*

I entered the restaurant and ignored the hard stares from the two elderly women in the corner. Yeah, they'd heard about what had happened. Everyone in Sleepy Creek had heard by now, and they sure weren't happy with me.

I sidled between the tables, feigning calm, and reached the counter after what seemed an eternity. "I'll take a chocolate shake to go, please."

"What are you doing here?" Grizzy asked.

Martin winced and backed off slowly. Jarvis glared out of the kitchen window, one maracas raised and a Mexican Fiesta Burger in a basket in his other hand.

"Just thought I'd drop by and see how things are going in my favorite restaurant."

Gosh, that had come out cheesy. And I matched it with a smile.

"Everything's fine," Griselda said. She whipped out the ingredients for the chocolate shake and set about making it. "You didn't have to, Chris."

"I know."

The terrible twins ogled me. Missi with downright anger, all pruned up, and Virginia with a blank expression. Neither gave me any comfort.

"Listen," I said, facing my friend again. "I feel really bad about what happened yesterday, Griz. I didn't want you to get involved."

"I could say the same thing about you."

I'd explained this to her. She knew that my mother's involvement in this had changed everything. She'd even hinted at me investigating the cold case when I'd first arrived. But there was a big difference between a closed case and an ongoing investigation.

"I don't know what to say other than I'm

sorry. I know you think I shouldn't stick my neck out but this is my—"

Grizzy switched on the blender and drowned me out. She concentrated on the silver cylinder and the wand, nothing else.

Had I lost the trust of my best friend because of this? She was the only person I had. I could afford to stay in one of Sleepy Creek's rundown motels, even if Grizzy claimed she wanted me to bunk in her guest room, but I didn't want to lose her after years of friendship.

Finally, the machine clicked off. She grabbed a takeaway cup and poured the shake into it. Popped the lid on top. Grabbed a straw and slid both across the counter toward me. I caught my reflection in the mirror behind the bar and grimaced.

"I don't want to lose you, Griz. OK?"

"I need time to be alone." Griselda sighed. "That's all. You're not losing me, and I'm not angry. I need to work and be on my own. I've got more to think about than just you, Chris.

The universe doesn't revolve around you and your cases."

That wasn't fair. And it was a little mean too.

"Just space. That's all. I'll talk to you this evening when I get home."

"This evening? You're going to work a full day?"

"Yeah, I need to."

I took the milkshake and patted my back pocket, grazing the outline of my wallet.

"On the house," Grizzy said.

"Thanks." Though, the only reason she'd given it to me was to get me out of the Burger Bar quicker. "Thanks for everything, Griz." I headed for the exit, cheeks burning from the attention I'd garnered—the twins in the corner, specifically. Missi let out a low hiss.

This had to be what the hunchback of Notre Dame felt like.

"It's my mother," I whispered, and clenched my free fist. It was *my* mother. And an innocent man, grumpy but innocent, had died because of her. Or because of me. How was I supposed to sit back when I'd spent the last ten years investigating murders back in Boston?

I could make all the excuses in the world, but the bottom line was I wasn't going to stop now, no matter how much Griz and the twins wanted me to. And that made me selfish. I got that.

This was a choice I'd made. Because when it came to my mother there wasn't a cold chance in heck I'd let it slide.

I squared my shoulders and set off down the street that led to Griselda's house, stomach churning.

❧   18   ❧

I sat at the kitchen table with my laptop open and scanned the search results on the Somerville Spiders. I'd already gone through it and filled a notepad's page with information about the group.

*Disbanded in 2004. Most of the group members arrested and in prison. Possible someone pulled the strings?* I tapped the nib of my pen next to that question mark. Something didn't add up here, yet I couldn't put my finger on what it was.

I brought the letter from Loopy Paul's

desk out of my pocket and unfolded it, scanned the lines of text again.

*Dear Paul,*

*I understand you're concerned for my safety but there's not much I can do right now. I've always appreciated your help but I have to deal with this on my own.*

*Let me be clear, it wouldn't be appropriate for you to get involved, no matter how much you want to help. My cases are mine alone.*

*I hope you and your sister are well.*

*Warmest Regards,*

*Detective Watson*

"Cases," I said. "What does she mean by that? Her cases are her own?" Did that mean she'd taken on a case in Sleepy Creek and Paul had been concerned for her safety? He'd clearly felt beholden to her for helping him out of a sticky situation back in Boston.

But if Paul was concerned about a Sleepy Creek case, that might rule out a Somerville Spider as a suspect. I couldn't exactly search for old murder cases in Sleepy Creek on my computer. It was unlikely I'd find any useful information on the internet.

I needed the actual case files. Perhaps, if I spoke with the Captain back in Boston I could get him to put in a word for me on this side, and then I could file a request for the information.

I dismissed that idea out of hand. I was already on thin ice with the Captain. If I let him know, even subtly, that I wanted to investigate during my imposed vacation he'd lose his donuts. And he loved his donuts.

I pushed my chair back and hustled over to the coffee pot, yawning. It was already past 6:00 p.m., and I hadn't had anything to eat. I didn't want to order takeout from Grizzy's Burger Bar. That would be awkward, given that Grizzy handled most home deliveries.

I poured myself a mug of coffee then glugged it back. "That's the stuff."

The doorbell tinkled—a merry tune.

I traipsed past Curly Fries, who'd set up

shop in the doorway, and she batted my ankle as I passed. "Who is it?" I called out.

"Miss Watson?" Balle's voice carried through the door.

What was it now? I opened up and stepped back to let him through. "Detective," I said. "I didn't expect to see you again so soon."

Liam didn't smile at me. "Uh-huh. I didn't expect to be here this soon either. I need to speak to you, Miss Watson. Do you have a minute?"

"I take it this is case related?"

"Yes."

I shut the door, locked it, then led him to the kitchen table. I grabbed the letter, folded it, and hid it in my pocket before he made it to his seat.

"What's going on?" I asked, and sat down opposite him. I shut the laptop's lid. He wouldn't realize what I'd researched was related to his case, but I didn't want to take the risk.

"I told you to stay out of this case, Watson," he said. "You've endangered yourself and your friend. Do you realize how serious that is?"

"What are you talking about?" We'd already had this discussion after Grizzy's arrest.

"You spoke to Frances Sarah Dawkins today. I got a distressed call from her down at the station. She thinks you're going to interfere in Paul's case to find out what happened to your mother. She's concerned that you're going to muddy the evidence. It took me a half an hour to reassure her."

So much for kindred spirits in pain.

"I—"

"She said you had a letter which mentioned her brother."

"I—"

"She said you were asking questions about the Somerville Spiders."

"Hey, wait a minute here. You're assuming all this stuff happened, and you haven't even heard my side of it." Pity my side of it would match what Frances had told him and get me into a mess of trouble.

"I don't want to hear excuses," Liam said. "At the beginning of this week I might've given you the benefit of the doubt, but you've proved again and again that you're determined to interfere in my investigation. Do you have any idea how frustrating that is?" His professional façade cracked and a sliver of anger peeked through.

"I didn't mean to frustrate you."

"It's a natural consequence of what you're doing, Christie." The first time he'd used my full name, and it sounded good. Weird that I'd pick up on that in the middle of being chewed out for my behavior. "I'm willing to wipe the slate clean if you offer up any physical and anecdotal evidence you might've found on your, uh, travels."

I didn't have much of a choice here. Frances had already outed me. Grizzy and the locals were angry at me for getting involved.

Liam was ready to explode beneath his perfectly ironed shirt.

Maybe, it was time to back off and let him handle this case. My stomach roiled. *But my mother is—*

I sighed. "Here," I said, and drew the letter out of my pocket.

I placed it on the table and slid it over. I ripped off the top page of my notepad and gave that to him next. "And here. That's all I've got."

Balle took both and read them. "These are interesting deductions," Liam said.

"Frances told me that my mother liberated them from the Somerville Spiders," I said. "And I figured if Paul wanted to give me information, then the only person who'd want to stop him was the person who murdered my mom. Or someone who was hired by that person. The Spiders went down because of her."

Liam folded up the letter again. "I'm afraid I'm going to have to take this."

"I understand." Of course, I understood.

Evidence was evidence and I'd had no right to withhold it. I would've handed it over eventually, of course, but that was my mother's handwriting. It was a tiny piece of her. Part of me had wanted to cling to that letter a little longer.

"Do you have any copies of this?" Liam asked.

"No," I replied.

"Good." He scraped his chair back. "Miss Watson, this is your final warning. If I catch you meddling again I'm going to arrest you. Don't make me do that, please."

I opened my mouth to reply, but he'd already left the kitchen. The front door clicked shut a few seconds later and left me in silence.

On the kitchen counter, the cordless phone started ringing.

❧ 19 ❧

"Hello?"

"H-hello! Hello, is that the noisy neighbor? The new girl?"

"Uh—who is this?" I asked, and leaned against the counter in Grizzy's kitchen. Curly Fries *prrt-meowed* and curled between my ankles, purring as if I was the one who fed her in the mornings.

"It's Ray," the guy said. "From next door?"

Right, the man who'd seen someone behind his house and told the cops about it. The cat hater who'd wielded a broomstick at the annoying feline now batting my trainers for attention. "Hi," I said. "Can I help you?"

"You're not outside."

An astute observation. "No, I'm indoors. Why do you ask?" And what business was it of his where I was or what I did?

"What about that Griselda woman? Is she there? She outside?"

"No. She's working late. Ray, I appreciate the call and everything, but could you tell me what's going on?"

"There's someone in my yard," he said.

"What?"

"There's. Someone. In. My. Yard. What are you, deaf?" Ray spat, but it was a show of bravado. His voice trembled around the edges, wobbly like a flan.

"Who?"

"It's Aqua-man," Ray said. "How am I supposed to know who it is, woman? That's why I'm calling you. It's the neighborly thing to do."

"Yes, warning me about homicidal maniacs

is at the top of the list." I sneaked to the kitchen window and clicked off the lights, plunging purring Curly Fries and myself into darkness.

"Who said anything about homicidal?"

I twitched the curtain aside and caught a view of Grizzy's empty yard. The cops had taken the seal off the back exit and rolled up the crime scene tape yesterday afternoon. "Why else would there be someone in your backyard?"

"Lady, you're giving me all kinds of goosebumps," Ray said.

"Do me a favor, Ray."

"I'm not big on favors."

"This one could save both our lives," I replied. The back fence remained sturdy, untouched—no dark shadows waxing or waning in front of it this time. Ray might've seen an animal or it was a trick of anxiety and shadows, but I wasn't prepared to take that risk given the circumstances.

"What is it?" Ray asked.

"Go to your kitchen window and tell me what you see."

The phone crackled—fabric on plastic—and a second of tense quiet intervened. "I'm here," Ray whispered. I could almost feel the heat of his breath through the receiver. "There's someone by my back fence."

"How tall?"

"Tall. Manly tall," he said.

I rolled my eyes. There were plenty of tall women. How did he know it wasn't Adriana Lima in his backyard? That would make Ray's life better. "Give me an estimate."

"I dunno, lady, six foot somethin'."

"What's the figure doing?"

Ray's breath whistled. "He's standing there. I think he's facing my back porch but I can't make it out. Hold on, let me switch on the porch light."

"No—"

Light flared next door, blocked by the slats of the fence—I could only make out the bulb and the gabled roof over it.

"Oh, he's just climbed over the top. He's wearing a coat. He's behind the fence."

"Can you make out which direction he's going?" I asked.

"Yeah, in your direction. I think he's coming to your house, but I can't see what's going on. I'm going to call the cops," Ray said.

"Don't," I replied.

"What? Why?"

"I'll, uh, I'll call them. Listen, Ray, lock yourself up in there. Stay safe."

"Don't gotta tell me twice." He hung up.

I placed the phone on the kitchen counter, but didn't shift focus from that back fence. It rattled, boards warping under pressure, and that shadowy figure appeared.

I didn't have a gun with me. Grizzy didn't carry, and mine had been confiscated—options for self-defense were limited. I grabbed Griselda's granite rolling pin and hefted it with a grunt, then unlocked the back door.

I opened it, praying the hinges wouldn't creak. They didn't. I slipped onto the porch and left the door open behind me, dropped into a crouch, and weighed my options.

A starless night coated the area in darkness. Rustles in the grass, the scent of cooking from the house over, and the gentle drip-drip of water somewhere nearby. I took it all in. The crickets had gone quiet.

Where was he? *Ah, there!*

Shadow man dropped down on my side of the fence and muttered under his breath. Not particularly stealthy behavior for a suspected murderer.

He hunched over and crept toward the porch.

One twitch and I'd reveal my position.

The figure reached the base of the stairs, straightened, and took them two at a time. He hit the porch and froze—must've spotted the open kitchen door. "Huh?"

I whipped the rolling pin around and rammed it into the backs of his knees. The wooden handle broke free.

"Oi!" The intruder pitched forward and

hit the deck with a bang that thundered through the house.

I leaped up and placed my foot on his back. "Don't move," I growled.

"Please, please, don't hurt me. Please!" A familiar voice broken by the shrill ring of the cordless phone on the kitchen counter. "Please!"

"What are you doing here?" I asked. "No, scratch that. Who are you?"

"It's Pete. Pete Dawkins. I came to talk."

The phone fell silent, but the ringing started up again instantly.

"Yeah, because climbing over fences screams friendly conversation." I took my foot off his back, then jogged inside and fetched the phone. "Yeah?" I answered.

"I heard a bang," Ray said.

I flicked on the kitchen lights and blinded my new "guest". He squinted up at me, pale around the lips and shaking. "Please don't kill me," he whispered.

"Everything's fine. It's Pete," I said.

"That charity idiot?"

"That's the one."

"Good luck," Ray said, and hung up again. *Ever the hero, our Ray.*

I put the phone down and followed suit with the rolling pin—I owed Grizzy a new one. Pete hadn't quit groaning or fumbling for the backs of his knees. I hadn't taken it easy on him. Why would I when he'd basically trespassed right after a man had been murdered in the back yard?

"Don't kill me," Pete repeated.

"Don't be ridiculous," I said. "Now, what do you want? And why didn't you call?"

"I didn't want anyone to know I was here. I—didn't want Sleepy Creek's Gossip Circle to hear."

There were too many questions to ask, and I couldn't get them out with Pete rolling around on the porch. I marched to his side and extended a hand. "Come in, then. You've got a lot of explaining to do."

Pete took my hand and scrambled to his

feet, wincing and whining. "You told Ray I'm here. Everyone's going to know. The whole of Sleepy Creek."

"So?"

"So, if they know then *he* will know."

"Who?" I asked, and closed up behind my limping guest.

"The murderer."

I locked the back door.

## 20

It took five minutes for Pete to calm down, and even then he jumped when I poured him a mug of coffee. That was my instant solution to every problem known to man. A cup of coffee a day kept the fear away.

"Let's start from the top," I said, and took the seat across from him. "You came out here to find who? Grizzy?"

"You," he said. "You're the out-of-towner, right? The new woman? I think I saw you at the Sleep Apnea event."

"That's right."

"I heard a rumor that you're involved in the case. That you're an undercover cop from the big city searching for the murderer," he said. "I figured I'd skip straight to the source."

I was tempted to let him live that illusion. Sanity prevailed this time. "I'm not an undercover cop working on the case," I said. "I'm a cop on sabbatical who came down to Sleepy Creek for the amenities." It was a bad joke, and Pete didn't catch it.

"Oh," he said. "Oh." And his shoulders drooped. "You're kidding."

"I'm afraid not," I said. "I'm investigating the case in a personal capacity, however. Paul knew my mother."

"Your mother?"

"Yes. My mother was murdered in Sleepy Creek twelve years ago."

"Holy fireballs," Pete muttered. "That's— I'm sorry about that."

I waved off the sympathy. "You've come all

this way. If you've got something to tell me, I'd appreciate hearing it."

It was almost 8:00 p.m., and Grizzy still hadn't come home. Did she plan on waiting until I was already asleep?

"All right," Pete said. "I'll have to tell the cops too, though. The real cops."

I bristled, but slammed the professional facade into place. "What happened?"

"Someone's watching my house," he said. "It makes my skin crawl saying it but I'm sure of it. It happens every night now."

"What does?"

"I hear noises in the forest. Scraping and banging. Someone out there in the night and they're taunting me. They want me to know they're after me," Pete said.

"But why?" Pete wasn't technically involved. Granted, his innocence hadn't been proven yet, and he had a potential motive for Paul's murder.

"I don't know. OK, I do. That's why I came," Pete said, and scanned the cat in the corner as if he expected Curly Fries to morph into a secret agent and pounce on him. "It happened about a month ago."

"What did?"

"The meeting. Paul was staying with me at the time because he didn't want to stay with Frances. They fought a lot. Everybody fought with Frances a lot." Pete snorted. "Anyway, Paul was a fine house guest. He didn't pry into my private business, you know? So, I was surprised when he came to me on a Friday and asked for my help."

"What help?"

"He wanted a ride to a specific place. Down by the old tracks on Herbert Road."

I arched an eyebrow. Herbert Road was the "bad" part of town—mom had warned me about the place when we'd first relocated to Sleepy Creek, and Griz had told me tales of the illegal dealings down by the tracks.

"Yeah," Pete said. "Yeah. Naturally, I was dubious. I didn't want to go down there. And it was colder than a witch's behind too."

"But you took him?"

"I did. I felt bad for Paul. He'd been acting strange all week, and I figured I'd help him out this once. You know, I wouldn't want him thinking he could take advantage of me whenever the fancy took him. But I had questions. I think I had too many questions. I asked him who he was meeting with and why, and he wouldn't give me a straight answer."

"What happened when you arrived?" I asked.

"He shot out of the car faster than a bullet leaves a gun. If you knew Paul it was quite a sight to behold, those arms and legs flailing around." Pete illustrated with his limbs. "I didn't see who he was meeting with because he made me park around the corner, but I did find this on his seat. I think he dropped it." Pete slid a slip of paper across the table.

"You've kept this an entire month?" I picked it up.

*G. B.—spot the tat.* A handwritten note. What on earth did it mean?

"I forgot about it until all this happened."

I descended into a fugue, mind swirling like a whirlpool above a plughole. G.B. What was G.B? No, who was G.B?

"Hello?" Pete rapped his knuckles on the table. "Can I get that back please? I should speak to Detective Balle about this."

"Yeah, you should," I said, and handed it over. Liam couldn't blame me for this, surely. The man had trespassed on private property and practically hunted me down to give me evidence in the case. So what if I'd egged him on a little? "And if you're concerned that someone's watching you, you should report that to him too and ask for protection."

"You're right," Pete said. "I'll do that. I should've done that first but—I, uh, I don't have the best history with the cops."

"Oh?"

"Nothing serious," he said, quickly. "Just minor infractions when I was younger. Got to go." He scraped his chair back and stumbled toward the back door.

"Not that way," I said. "I'll let you out the front."

"I don't want him to see me."

"No one's watching except my nosy neighbor Ray, and he already knows you're here." I escorted him to the exit, Curly Fries tinkling along behind us, and unlocked the door. "You take care."

"You too." Pete scurried down the stairs and into the night.

Why would Pete have approached an undercover police officer if he was afraid of the cops? Or wary of them? Had he run into trouble with Liam, specifically? And who or what was G.B.?

Plots drifted up from the depths. Loopy Paul involved with the mafia again. His sister funneling money through the charity—it would explain the expensive car and clothes. "No," I whispered.

Too much conjecture. The night had marched on and I'd been left to my own devices for too long. What worried me the most about this was the fact that Griselda still hadn't arrived.

Curly Fries meowed at me.

"I know," I said. "I know, I'm an idiot. I should put this Paul and mom stuff aside." The cat gave me a yellow-eyed stare that pierced my soul. Missi's tease about kitty cannibalistic tendencies came back to me. I bent and patted her on the head. "See you later. Don't poop in your kibble."

Waiting for Grizzy to get home would drive me crazy. We *had* to talk this out.

## 21

I rat-tatted my knuckles on the glass door of the Burger Bar, then let myself in. Missi and Virginia were at their booth, and a couple of the other regulars were finishing up the remains of their burgers.

I ignored them. Griselda had already taken out the register's tray and was packing the money into plastic bags that would go into the safe. It was a sign of Sleepy Creek's supposed level of safety that she did it with customers still in the store.

It helped that she had cameras in the corners too. I squished onto one of the puffy 50s diner-style stools. "Hey," I said. "How's the day treated you?"

Grizzy shrugged. "Fine, I guess. I haven't had much time to think. It was super busy today, which is a good thing."

"Night, Griselda!"

The two elderly women twiddled their fingers at my friend. Missi regarded me with suspicion. "You take care," she said, directing it at Griz.

What, did my own friend need protection from me?

"Night ladies," Griselda replied.

They swept out the door and clanged it shut behind them. Only two regulars remained at tables on opposite ends of the room. The kitchen was dark and empty— Jarvis had already left for the night.

"I don't suppose it will help if I apologize again," I said.

"No."

"You're never open this late. I was worried about you."

Griselda had a "no burgers after 8:00 p.m." rule. Partly because it was a small town and she could get away with it as the only supplier of delicious meaty treats, and partly because most people avoided going out in the cold after the sun had set.

"You didn't need to worry. Like I said, I needed time to be alone. I've got a lot to think about."

"What else is bothering you?"

"Just that stuff we talked about this week."

I lowered my voice. "Arthur?"

"Yeah. And the fact that there was a murder on my property. You arrived and a storm of strangeness hit Sleepy Creek. And not the regular strangeness you get around here."

I resisted the urge to apologize. My arrival may or may not have sparked off Loopy Paul's actions, but that didn't make me directly responsible. Did it?

"You realize that's why I did everything I've done? There's a murderer out there, and from what I've heard, they might be closer than we realize."

"Meaning?" Griselda placed the plastic bags of cash neatly in the tray, then made for the office.

I followed.

Finally, Grizzy wanted to hear what I had to say about the case instead of lecturing me about how I shouldn't get involved. This had to be a breakthrough.

We entered Griselda's tiny office, decorated with furniture I recognized from the house, the pieces her mom had kept in the guest room when we'd been in high school.

"I had a visit this evening," I said. "It was technically an almost break-in. Which reminds me, I've got to get you a new rolling pin. I loosened the handle on your one at home."

"What?" Grizzy fiddled with the dial on the safe in the corner. "But you don't cook."

"I wasn't cooking when I loosened it. Anyway, Pete Dawkins came to see me. He thought I was investigating the case as an undercover cop. That's a rumor that's going around town."

"Wow," Grizzy said, and gave a doleful sigh. "Small town syndrome."

I cleared my throat, raised my hands like an orchestra conductor and launched into the details of Pete's visit. Grizzy shut the safe and led me back into the restaurant, gasping or "oohing" at the appropriate parts of my story.

"And then he gave me this note," I said. "And get this—wait, should I even tell you about this when you're still mad at me for investigating?"

Griselda laughed. "I was never mad at you. Just disappointed that you don't look out for your own best interests. So yeah, you can talk to me about it, but on one condition."

"What?"

"You don't get involved in any other investigations while you're in Sleepy Creek."

"What about my mo—"

"Apart from that," she said. "Deal?"

I didn't have to consider it. "Deal."

It wasn't as if there was a murder a week in Sleepy Creek. *Hey, that rhymed.*

"Right, so what did Pete give you?" Grizzy asked.

I took a second to admire my friend's pragmatism. If Arthur couldn't see what an awesome person she was, he had to be blind. "He gave me a slip of paper that Paul dropped in his car."

"What did it say?"

"It said, *G.B.—spot the tat.*"

"Huh?"

"Exactly." I sat down on my stool again. "It's either a person or a place. I've thought it over, and I haven't come up with anything except that it has to be someone's initials."

"A tat. Like a tattoo?"

"Yeah," I said. "A tattoo." The skin on the back of my neck prickled, and I lurched off my seat. "A tattoo! G.B. No, it can't be."

George Brighton. The hand tattoo guy. The man I'd served burgers to several times this week, who sat in a particular spot in the restaurant. He barely talked. And the tattoo on his hand had been a bug or a... a... "Spider."

"What are you talking about?" Grizzy asked.

"Griz, there's a guy that's been coming in here for the past week or so. He eats a Mexican Fiesta Burger every day and sits at the table in the center of the room. He's a regular."

"What? No. That guy's new. In fact, I don't think he came in before the start of this week," she said, and her eyes went burger bun round. "Wait a second, you don't think—"

A chair clattered to the linoleum behind me. I froze. We'd been so caught up in the moment we'd forgotten about the two others in the store and now, we'd either started a wildfire rumor about the youngster who'd eaten in here, or we'd scared the pants off of some old burger-loving lady.

"Chris," Grizzy whispered, and the color faded from her cheeks. "C-Christie."

"Don't move a muscle." Breath whistled in my ear and pain pricked at the base of my spine. Pressure against my cotton shirt—a knife?

Grizzy glanced at the cameras.

"If you do anything stupid, I'll slice her, understand?" The man's voice was cold and hard.

Griselda nodded.

I turned my head ever so slightly and caught sight of the man in my peripherals. George Brighton had been in the restaurant all along.

❧ 22 ❧

"You're too young," I said.

"What?" George increased the pressure of the blade against my back. "What did you say?"

"You killed Paul because of the picture. You're part of the Somerville Spiders," I said, "but you're too young to have killed my mother."

"Shut up." George grabbed my arm and twisted it behind my back. "You shut up or I'll give you an extra hole to breathe out of."

I didn't doubt he would, under the right

circumstances, but this wasn't a dark back-yard. Griselda was here as a witness. There were cameras in here, which George had to know about since he'd eaten here all week.

Why then? Did he plan on holding us hostage? Making demands? That had to be it.

He wanted a plea deal, no doubt. He wanted the DA to go easy on him, and murdering two women wouldn't get him that.

"Who paid you?" I asked.

"Chris, stop," Grizzy whimpered. "He's got a knife."

"Yes, I'm aware of that, Griselda." It was pressed against me, after all. An icy calm washed over me.

"Who paid you?"

George jerked me around and led me to one of the booths. He flung me into it, then pointed at Grizzy, who'd shifted an inch to her right, toward the kitchen.

"Get over here," he said, and pressed the knife to my throat this time. "Now."

Griselda scooted toward us, but tripped and caught herself on the counter. "Oomph!"

"Hurry up," George snapped.

"Easy," I said. "Easy, man, she fell."

"You shut your trap!" The guy trembled, adrenaline driving him closer to the edge. I had to get him back before he crossed over and decided we weren't worth the trouble. Or that he didn't care what those cameras caught.

Griselda streaked across the restaurant and sat down opposite me in the booth.

Brighton finally lifted the knife from my neck, but didn't stow it. "Here's what's going to happen," he said. "You two ladies are going to sit nice and quiet, like ladies should, and I'm going to take what I need from the register and leave."

"I've already emptied the register," Grizzy said. "It's all in the safe."

George ground his teeth. "What's the safe code?"

"I—well, it's a little complicated. You have

to wiggle the dial to get it to work," she said. "I could do it for you."

"No. You might have a gun in there or somethin'. I don't trust you."

"Who *do* you trust?" I asked. "I know you killed Paul. But why? Because he was about to tell me about my mother? Why would you care?" And how could he be a part of the Somerville Spiders? He had to have been twelve-years-old when they'd disbanded.

"I told you to shut up," George replied.

"It's a Spider isn't it?" I nodded to the tattoo on his knife-wielding hand. I'd already figured out the answer, but I wanted him to talk. The minute he relaxed I'd have a shot at disarming him.

Neither of us could call the cops on the guy.

George scratched his tattoo. "Quiet."

I scanned him. Slight lean to the left. He favored that side. An old injury?

He had to have been paid off to get rid of Paul. Paid off by the Spiders. Except the mafia hadn't officially been linked to my mother's death. That would've made the news.

None of the information burbling through me mattered as much as making sure that we got out of this safe.

I latched onto the only option I had left. "George, you're not to blame here. I know that you were paid to kill Paul."

He didn't speak, but he didn't tell me to shut up either.

"And, if you did it on someone else's dime, there's a chance the cops will want to talk to you about that before they have you arraigned. You might be able to strike a deal, understand?"

"What would you know?" George asked, and the first sign of weakness showed through. He ran grubby fingers through his orange, tufty hair. "You're a waitress."

"I'm a police officer," I replied, coolly. "From Boston." If he ended up reporting back to whoever must've hired him he'd let them know these facts, and that was exactly what I wanted. To send a warning. I was here, and I was on it.

It would up the pressure, make the person who'd done it more likely to slip up.

"You're—"

"That's right. I know what's going to happen to you, George. And I know that you'll only make things worse for yourself if you harm either of us, understand?"

Sirens screamed in the distance, shrill whoops chased by the reflection of flashing blue and red lights in the windows of the store opposite. The cavalry had arrived. But how?

George shifted his weight and winced. "You called the cops."

"No," I replied. "But it's over now, Mr. Brighton. You have to realize that."

"It's not over until I say so." He dove for me, knife outstretched, lips peeled back over yellowed teeth.

I raised my forearm and deflected the blow. Hit him on the wrist. I launched myself out of the booth and tackled him to the ground, tugging left.

He landed on his sore side. I rolled onto his knife-wielding arm. "Stop right there," I yelled.

George wheezed and raised his right fist.

I had nothing to protect from the blow, my left arm pinning his to the ground. My right scrabbling with his fingers, trying to pry the knife free. My stomach knotted up—this was it.

"Freeze, scumbag." A strong, tanned hand closed around Brighton's wrist.

I squinted up at my savior, Detective Liam Balle. The fear drained from my limbs.

"George Brighton, you're under arrest for the murder of Paul Whitmore. You have the right to remain silent," he said, his gun aimed right at George's head. "Anything you say, can and will be used against you in a court of law. You have the right to—"

I sat up, dragged my butt from the scene,

then rested my back against the side of the booth's cushy chair.

That was that. George had been arrested for the murder. He'd done all but admitted it in front of Grizzy and me before—

"Grizzy," I whispered, and pitched onto my knees. The booth was empty and Grizzy stood beside it, Arthur Cotton's arm wrapped around her shoulders, her head resting against his chest.

The sight should've brought a smile, but I couldn't relax. This wasn't over yet. This was far from over. George Brighton glared at me over his shoulder, hands behind his back now, bound by cuffs.

That stare would stay with me for the rest of my stay in Sleepy Creek.

## 23

George Brighton's spider tattoo had destroyed any chance I'd had of leaving Sleepy Creek with my reputation intact. He was a Somerville Spider, and I couldn't let that go. Not through the statement that Liam had taken, kind-eyed and concerned, nor through the long silent drive home in the back of Arthur Cotton's police car.

It was over. Paul's murderer had been caught and would be placed behind bars. Detective Balle had hinted that they'd been onto him before the showdown in the Burger Bar, and I believed him.

The letter I'd handed over had likely pointed them in the right direction, and they had access to information and files I didn't.

Arthur paraded us into the kitchen, clucking in the perfect imitation of a mother hen. I didn't doubt the concern was for Griselda—the real savior of the hour. She'd hit the panic button under the counter when she'd fake stumbled in the restaurant. That had alerted the alarm company, and given the location of that alert and the recent murder, they had let the cops know too.

I set about making us a pot of coffee while she saw Cotton out and assured him, for the millionth time, that we were OK. Curly Fries entered the kitchen and let off a terrific meow. I jumped. "You trying to give me a heart attack?"

"Don't blame the cutie kitty," Grizzy said, and bustled in. "She must be starving. I usually give her a nighttime top up before bed."

It was already past 12:00 a.m.. Statements had taken ages—and Arthur had been worried that the paramedics at the scene would hurt Griselda more than help her.

"Well." I clicked the switch on the coffee machine. "That was a fun night."

"It all happened so fast." Grizzy poured kibble into Curly's bowl. "I think I'm still in shock."

"Don't say that too loudly. Arthur might hear you and sprint back."

Griselda blushed. "He was so sweet. He was worried about me."

"I hadn't noticed it. I mean, it wasn't obvious apart from every second word he breathed was your name."

"Stop," Griz said, and drew the word out. "He was nice. And he hinted that he wanted to talk to me tomorrow. I don't know what he wants, but it's got me nervous."

"That's got you nervous," I said. "Never mind the fact we almost *died* tonight."

"Don't remind me." Griselda put the bag

of kibble back in the cupboard—at the top in case Curly Fries got any wise ideas—then sat down at the table and rubbed her eyes. "Wow, that was intense."

"You can say that again."

"Wow, that was—"

"Lame." I cuffed her on the shoulder. "And I think we both know exactly what Arthur's going to ask you."

"We do?" Grizzy didn't turn around.

Arthur wanted to ask her out. If anything would spur the man on it had to be a near death experience for Griz.

"He's obviously going to ask you on a date," I said. "And I've got to say, I'll breathe a sigh of relief when he does. I think it's been a long time coming. That's the rumor in the restaurant."

Griselda dropped her hands. "What rumor?"

A knock saved me from answering. I left for the entrance hall.

"What rumor?" Grizzy called after me.

The knock came again, followed by two hushed voices on the other side of Grizzy's front door.

"They're definitely home," a woman said.

"Yeah, you don't say. The lights are on. Why aren't they answering?"

"The poor dears are terrified after what happened. We should let them know they're safe."

"Well, yeah, that's what we're trying to do right—"

I unlocked the door and opened it on Sleepy Creek's terrible twins. Virginia and Missi stood side-by-side, both outfitted in their pajamas—two robes, one lilac and the other baby blue, tied at the waist.

"Took you long enough," Missi said, and trudged past me.

"Sorry, dear, we don't mean to be rude. We were worried about you. We heard about George Brighton and the arrest." Virginia patted my forearm and followed her sister into the house. "Griselda, dear?"

"She's in the kitchen," Missi yelled back.

I locked up again, then followed the duo. They'd already taken up seats at the kitchen table.

"Are you two all right?" Missi asked, gruffly. "We thought we'd lost you for a second there."

"I'm touched," I said. "You care what happens to us."

"Of course I care," Missi replied. "Where else would I get my milkshakes if Grizzy's Burger Bar went under?"

"She's joking, of course. We're utterly relieved you're all right." Virginia stroked the back of Griselda's hand. "Are you shaken up, dear?"

"No, I'm fine. We're both fine," Griz said. "But I *am* starving."

"I don't think takeout is an option at this time of night."

"Takeout, pah," Missi said, and rolled up the sleeves of her lilac robe. "I'll whip us up a delicious treat in no time. Let me see what's in the fridge." She rose and crossed to the silver monster in the corner, opened it, then practically disappeared inside.

Virginia tut-tutted. "I can't believe it was George. He's always been a bit of a question mark, but to do this—"

"Wait, always been? He's been in town longer than a week?"

"Oh, yes," Virginia said. "Yes, he was born in Sleepy Creek. I believe he left a few years back, but returned about a month ago."

"Where did he work?" I asked.

"At the old station," Virginia said.

"The train tracks," I whispered. "Of course." But the knowledge didn't get me any closer to the truth about my mother's case. Hopefully, George would talk in the interrogation room and give the cops a lead. I was doubtful, though.

"Any idea why he did it?" Virginia asked.

Griz and I exchanged a glance. Did I want these two women to know about my mother and the Somerville Spiders? Would it endanger them if they knew? Griz gave a tiny shake of her head. I couldn't help agreeing with the sentiment.

Virginia and Missi were sweet. They didn't deserve the drama that went with what had happened this week. "Not a clue," Griz said, at last.

"What about you?" Virginia asked.

"Don't know and don't want to know. I'm done sticking my nose where it doesn't belong." *Lies. All lies.*

Virginia hummed under her breath—and if I wasn't mistaken she was a little... disappointed. But that couldn't be right, could it?

"Oh, wonderful, you have chicken fillets," Missi said, and saved me from having to lie, outright. "How about fajitas?"

"Sounds like heaven to me," Griselda said.

I tuned out the unease and focused on the moment. A week had passed since I'd arrived in Sleepy Creek, and I'd already picked up two new, albeit reluctant, friends. This place felt like home again.

The case of the loopy dead man had been solved. My mother's hadn't been. And I'd learned a valuable lesson: try as I might, I couldn't avoid the past. It had caught up with me.

For now, I could sit back, relax and enjoy this moment in Griselda's kitchen, teasing Griz about Arthur Cotton and joking about Curly Fries' unbelievable appetite.

Tomorrow was another day. I couldn't wait for what it would bring.

*Christie's story continues in the second book in the Burger Bar Mystery Series, The Double Cheese Burger is out now! Click here to get it.*

# CRAVING MORE COZY MYSTERY?

**If you had fun with Christie, you'll want to meet Milly and her pet bunny Waffle. You can read the first chapter of Milly's story below!**

"It's unheard of! A travesty." My grandmother, Cecelia Pepper, sat on the edge of her seat at the coffee bar in the Starlight Cafe. "Why, the sheriff ought to be ashamed of himself. How are we meant to walk down the streets in this town with this... threat in the backs of our minds? Looming! Like some giant Sword of

Damocles over our heads." She tapped the newspaper, a copy of *The Star Lake Gazette*, she'd laid on the coffee bar the minute she'd sat down.

My grandmother was the definition of dynamite in a small package. At 75-years-old, she was brimming with vigor to make up for her height.

"I'm sure Sheriff Rogers will figure it out." I fixed Gran a cup of coffee—a hazelnut latte with extra cream—and placed it in front of her. "It's a small town, Gran. They'll catch whoever's doing this."

"A small town that's going downhill quickly." My grandmother glanced around as if she was afraid of someone overhearing our conversation.

But the painful truth was there was nobody in my cafe this morning. Just like there'd been nobody in it the day before.

As I'd learned quickly, folks in Star Lake, Iowa, were insular. They didn't care that my late father, a town favorite, had left me the cafe. I hadn't lived in town long enough for them to trust me, and then there was the fact that I had absolutely no experience in the hospitality industry.

*Not now. Just take a breath and smile.*

"I mean, really. A mugger? Here? Nancy from the bakery told me her sister's best friend's cousin was attacked. Wallet stolen. Can you believe that? If I didn't love the lake and the people so much," my grandmother continued, lifting the latte, "I'd move away in a heartbeat."

"Gran."

"I'm serious."

"Gran, you've lived here for thirty-five years."

"Fine. I might not move, but I'll protest this at the next town council meeting. You can mark my words on that." Gran took a sip of her latte, pressed her lips together and fluttered her eyelashes. "Nearly as good as your father used to make."

A silence ensued, filled with our shared

sorrow. It was too soon to talk about him.

I cast my gaze away from Gran and studied the interior of the cafe. Light streamed through the windows and the glass front doors, illuminating the linoleum that was in need of a revamp, as well as the checked tablecloths and laminated menus. The chairs were comfortable and well worn. The cash register was an antique and the walls were dark wood.

Overall, the aesthetic was typical of my dad's taste. Hastily thrown together but with plenty of heart.

"This really is good." Gran must've noticed the lump in my throat. Metaphorically, of course. "You know, you'll make a fine restaurant owner. As fine an owner as you would've made a detective."

That was another touchy subject. "Thanks, Gran." I forced a smile.

She reached over and patted my forearm.

Movement outside on the brick-paved sidewalk caught my attention. A homeless woman, wearing a shabby coat and carrying several plastic bags, walked up and took a seat outside the cafe.

"Oh dear," Gran said.

"Do you know her?"

"Only by sight," Gran replied. "She's new to town I think. I'm not familiar with her story. Poor woman."

I bit down on my lip then headed back to the coffee machine and started fixing another latte. Much to my surprise, the bell over the door tinkled, and Sheriff Rogers entered.

He was in his late fifties, with a gray mustache, balding, and wearing his uniform with pride. He sauntered over to the bar and eyed me. "Morning."

"Good morning, Sheriff," I said. "What can I get for you today?"

The sheriff didn't immediately answer me. He scanned the interior of the cafe then pointed over to a new section I'd set up, with the help of my cook, Francesca. "What's that?"

"That's the waffle station," I said, smiling. "Do you want to try it out? We prepare the waffles fresh, bring 'em out to you, and then you decorate them as you see fit. There's ice cream and maple syrup, there's—"

"That wasn't here when Frank was running the place."

"No," I said. "No, it wasn't. I figured that people would enjoy—"

"Waffles?"

"Sheriff Rogers," my grandmother said, and the sheriff jumped a little.

"Celia." He sniffed, using Gran's nickname. "Shoot. I didn't see you there." And he sounded truly regretful, like he was anticipating a volley of complaints. He wouldn't have been wrong in that respect.

"What's this I hear about a mugger?" Gran tapped the newspaper. "A mugger in our midst?"

"Well, yeah, there have been reports of muggings over the past week, but I assure you it's under control."

"Now, Sheriff, you know better than to shovel that level of manure around me," Gran said. "I want answers, and I want them now. What am I supposed to tell the ladies in my book club? That we can't walk to the library in peace?"

"I assure you…"

The conversation faded out as I finished off the latte, grabbed a cupcake from the display of about a dozen under the glass counter, and walked out into the sunlight.

It was the end of summer, the weather a temperate 70 degrees with a soft breeze brushing down the street. I stopped in front of the homeless woman.

"Good morning," I said.

She glared at me, her skin tan, and her ire obvious. "What do you want, Red?"

The urge to brush my fingers through my red hair nearly overtook me. Thankfully, my hands were full. "Uh."

"Let me guess. You want me to move. It's a free country, you know, I—"

"No," I said. "I just wanted to check if you were OK."

"OK?"

"Yeah." I handed her the coffee and the cupcake. "You need anything?" It was my experience, after working as a beat cop in the city, that everyone had a story. Just like everyone had a purpose. Sometimes life just… got in the way.

The woman blinked. "Uh. Yeah. I'm good. Thanks."

"Sure. Just holler if you need a glass of water or something," I said. "I'll be inside."

The woman, still full of mistrust, nodded then took a sip of her coffee. I headed back into the cafe and found Gran and Sheriff Rogers embroiled in their argument.

"—muggers on the streets. If you think that we'll stand for this then you're delusional. You know, I can call up the heads of the three factions, right now, and get them to arrange a meeting."

Sheriff Rogers, blustery as he was, paled at that.

The "factions" as they were called, were the three unions that pretty much ran Star Lake. There were "the boaters", "the butchers", and "the bakers"—and they frequently disagreed on issues, to the point where the town was practically split into three. It was expected that you'd fall into line with one of the groups even if you weren't an active member of said union.

"The bakers would be most interested to hear about your lack of action when it comes to crime on our streets. I mean, this whole area is packed with bakeries and restaurants. This is bound to affect tourism too. And then the boaters will get antsy."

The summer months in Star Lake were famed for their fun boating activities, from tours on the lake, to fishing, to jet skiing and recreational activities.

"You're complaining about mugging and crime on the street," Sheriff Rogers said, finding his voice, "yet you won't stop your granddaughter over here from feeding said criminals."

Gran jerked back as if she'd been slapped—a strange effect on a tiny woman in a floral-print dress. "Feeding them? I think the heat is getting to you, Sheriff."

"She just took out a coffee and a cupcake to..." He trailed off and gestured toward the homeless woman now sitting on a bench out front.

"And so?" Gran grew red and rose from her barstool, trying to tower at four feet eight inches.

The sheriff tugged on his collar. "All I'm saying is that if you don't want trouble, don't invite it into your home." And with that, he swept from the cafe, trailing his overbearing spicy cologne.

"Idiot," Gran muttered.

"Gran."

"There's no love lost between us." She resumed her seat. "And for good reason."

But she didn't go into the reason. I fixed a cup of coffee for Francesca, who was in the kitchen, patiently awaiting orders that would likely never come, and then joined my grandmother at the counter.

Gran paged through the newspaper, stopping on an image and tapping it. "See, now, this is why you don't want to get on the wrong side of those boaters. Look at that. A full page ad for their 'Boating Blowout 2021.'"

I read over her shoulder. "Join us for a boating extravaganza as we celebrate the end of summer."

"You're going, I assume? Everyone's going," Gran said. "Everybody who's anybody. It will be a great opportunity for you to network, dear. It's been a year, and you've only made one friend."

"Thanks, Gran."

"I'm just saying," she replied, "that it might be a good opportunity for you to get out there and meet someone."

"Meet someone? The only person I'm interested in meeting is an accountant who can help me manage my finances for this place." Things were *not* looking good. And I was *not* about to let down my father's legacy by losing the Starlight Cafe.

"I'm sure there are plenty of eligible accountants around."

"Not what I meant, Gran."

She gave me a sneaky smile, and it cheered me up. I couldn't stay mad at Gran.

"Are you coming by tonight for supper?" Gran asked. "I'm making chicken casserole. You can bring Waffle along."

"That sounds great."

It sure beat eating a microwave dinner over the kitchen sink.

Want to read more? You can grab **the first book** in THE MILLY PEPPER MYSTERY SERIES in paperback at your favorite retailer.

Happy reading, friend!

*Macarons and Murder*

*Candy Cake Murder*

*Murder by Rainbow Cake*


<u>*A Milly Pepper Mystery series*</u>

*Maple Drizzle Murder*


<u>*A Sunny Side Up Cozy Mystery series*</u>

*Murder Over Easy*

*Muffin But Murder*

*Chicken Murder Soup*

*Murderoni and Cheese*

*Lemon Murder Pie*


<u>*A Gossip Cozy Mystery series*</u>

*The Case of the Waffling Warrants*


<u>*A Mission Inn-possible Cozy Mystery series*</u>

*Vanilla Vendetta*

*Strawberry Sin*

*Cocoa Conviction*

*Mint Murder*

*Raspberry Revenge*

*Chocolate Chills*